Readers love
SCOTTY CADE

Forever For Now

"Scotty Cade is usually good for a sweet low-angst story with a guaranteed happily ever after, and *Forever for Now* is no exception."
—Prism Book Alliance

"…a good choice if you are looking for a quick, sexy read. You'll enjoy the heroes' chemistry and it has an ending that will leave a smile on your face."
—Top 2 Bottom Reviews

Final Encore

"It's quick and sweet, and sure to appeal to fans of country music and rags-to-riches tales."
—Joyfully Reviewed

"If you are a fan of country music this would be a good book to read! If you are a Scotty Cade fan, you'll probably like this one."
—Love Bytes Reviews

Knobs

"I really did like this story… If you are a fan of young love stories, you've got to check this one out!"
—Joyfully Jay

"Scotty Cade's *Knobs* is a well written and informative story about the Citadel Military College."
—The Novel Approach

By SCOTTY CADE

Acting Out
Forever for Now
Knobs
Losing Faith
The Mystery of Ruby Lode
Sunrise Over Savannah • Chasing the Horizon
An Unconventional Courtship • An Unconventional Union

BISSONET & CRUZ INVESTIGATIONS
The Royal Street Heist
Veiled Loyalties

FINAL ENCORE
Before the Final Encore
Final Encore
After the Final Encore

LOVE SERIES
Wings of Love
Bounty of Love
Treasure of Love
With Z.B. Marshall: Foundation of Love

Published by DREAMSPINNER PRESS
www.dreamspinnerpress.com

First and foremost, this book is dedicated to my husband, Kell. He's my true soul mate and has never wavered in his complete encouragement and never-ending support. Twenty-one years later and I still feel just as blessed as I did the day we met. I love you with all my heart.

This book is also dedicated to anyone who is struggling with sexual identification, loneliness, addiction, isolation, depression, or any other negative thoughts or feelings. The darkest of nights can seem cold and lonely, and you may feel lost and alone, but there is always someone out there who can help you awaken to a brand new dawn. Cullen found Abel, and if you reach out, someone will find you as well.

And lastly, if you see someone in need, please reach out. Don't let fear or intimidation hinder your natural instinct to help. Trust me when I say if you don't, it will stay with you forever.

PREFACE

HI, ALL. Scotty Cade here. Well, I've got to say I'm a little nervous about this one. This story deals with religion, faith, and the power of our dreams to help guide us to things that are right in front of our faces.

I normally shy away from religion as subject matter because it is such a personal thing, but this book called to me so strongly, I couldn't not write it. The story was inspired by a single moment in time. One instant when two virtual strangers made decisions that altered their lives. A personal encounter that stayed with me for weeks until I had no choice but to write the book.

The only difference in my encounter versus the one in the book is that the fictional character did the right thing where I lacked the courage—a decision I will regret for the rest of my life.

Here's how it went. Kell and I were on our boat on our yearly trek down south and had just arrived in a little town called Southport, NC. It's really a charming town, and we planned on staying there until December, before we moved farther south to Charleston. So after eight days on the water from Martha's Vineyard, we were very excited to finally be there.

On our first morning, at dawn, I went for my usual five-mile run and chose a route that took me along the Historic Southport Riverwalk. It was a beautiful morning, and the sun was just above the horizon, causing the dew on the grass to sparkle like little diamonds. I remember it so clearly.

I was running along at my usual pace, enjoying my solitude with no one else in sight, when I saw a man sitting on a park bench quite a distance ahead of me. Even from my vantage point, his body language seemed ominous and overwhelmed. His elbows were resting on his knees, and he was staring blankly out over the Cape Fear River. As I got closer, I saw the man was extremely handsome, well-groomed, clean-cut, and very well-dressed in a crisp white shirt, dark slacks, and a tie. The type of guy one might describe as metrosexual. And he was holding a book and rubbing his thumb gently over its cover.

Then the man moved his book a certain way, the sun reflected off of something gold, and I knew in my heart he was holding the Bible. The man really looked like he needed a friend. All sorts of possibilities ran through my head. Death. Depression. Illness. He was clearly struggling with something. I continued running toward him, trying to decide if I should stop, but I looked around, and there was no one except the two of us in the park. There were plenty of open park benches and swings overlooking the river, so I could think of no good reason to stop at his particular bench. In addition, I was fearful if I stopped, he might think I was trying to rob him—or even worse trying to pick him up. So therein lay my dilemma. Take a chance on being considered a pervert or stop to help someone who might be in need.

I think you know where this is going. Unfortunately, I didn't have the courage to stop, and I ran right past the guy. Truly, I don't think he even saw me as he was so deep in thought. I did greet him as I passed, but if I got a response, I didn't hear it.

When I got back to the boat, I told Kell and the friends who were on board with us about my experience, and they seemed unaffected, but the encounter stayed with me all day and night. The next morning, I ran again. The same time and the same route. And I've done that every day we've been here—over a month. But I never saw the stranger again. Of course, this sent my mind into a tizzy of guilt. Was the guy sick? Or, even worse, was he so distraught he took his own life? All these ideas plagued me and stayed with me. Even after I started this book.

Just know, although I am a very spiritual person, I'm not a particularly religious one. I have my own personal relationship with the man upstairs, but I'm not a fan of organized religion. In my humble opinion, organized religion sometimes gives a certain group of people the right to discriminate against others who are not like them in the name of their God. Those of us in the LGBTQ community have most recently seen this regarding the right to marry. I won't give this woman any more publicity by mentioning her name, but you know to whom I'm referring. On the flip side, sometimes organized religion helps people be accepting of others. So there. I'm trying to be diplomatic.

Anyway, this book focuses on two very different denominations. The Episcopal Church and the Southern Baptist Church. I did a lot of research on both, and apart from their mutual love of the Gospel, they have very little in common. The Episcopalians welcome everyone to worship. They even ordain women and gay men as priests and bishops, while on the other hand, the Southern Baptists do not believe in women as ordained ministers and believe homosexuality is a grave sin. In fact, if you are gay, you will only be welcomed into the church if you denounce your homosexual desires and seek their help to change your sexual orientation through prayer and fellowship.

Now this is generalizing the denominations, and the last thing I want to do is offend, but for the record, I got all my information from the Southern Baptist Convention's official website and the Episcopal Church's official website. Their beliefs are clearly written there, and all you need to do is google either to see what I mean.

However, the next part of the book delves into the power of our dreams. Many people believe dreams are an open doorway to our souls, a way for our lost loved ones to communicate with us. And... I just happen to be one of those people.

But many others believe dreams are just our subconscious validating things we want to believe. Things like getting one last look at a lost loved one or simply knowing they are okay and have moved on. Things along those lines. In addition, when some people dream of a tragedy, they take it as a sign and try to avoid a certain situation, while others simply dismiss it as a nightmare triggered by something they saw on television or something someone said. In this book, one character's dreams are portals, for lack of a better word, for a lost loved one to come back and try to help him move on with his life.

I hope you take all of this as it is meant. The story is one of loss, identity, hypocrisy, need, and love. Writing it has helped me gain a little closure by giving my characters the happy ending I so hope my stranger enjoyed and easing my guilt a little for not stopping to help a fellow man in need.

Also, Kell and I loved Southport so much, I thought I would include a few photos so you can get a feel for the town's charm and the locations I wrote about.

I hope you enjoy!

Scotty

Southport, North Carolina

Southport Baptist Church

Southport Historic Riverwalk

Angels descending bring from above
Echoes of mercy, whispers of love.
Watching and waiting, looking above,
Filled with His goodness, lost in His love.

—*Fanny J. Crosby, Blessed Assurance*

CHAPTER ONE

WHAT STUPIDITY!

A Cabo sports fishing yacht had just blown past him at top speed, creating a massive, unpredictable, and potentially devastating wake. Cullen Kiley sucked in a ragged breath and tightened his grip on the steering wheel. While he prepared for the impact of the tsunami-like wave, Cullen said a prayer for the tiny houseboat off his starboard bow, which was surely going to be swamped. He didn't know why he prayed. Out of habit, he guessed.

On the Intracoastal Waterway, everyone was responsible for their own wake, so most boaters were kind, courteous, and offered nice slow passes to smaller boats. But not this guy. He was blowing past every boat on the busy waterway, literally leaving pandemonium in his wake.

Cullen had little time to do anything but cut into the large waves and hope for the best. The first wave smashed against his hull, the impact sending *T-Time*, his forty-eight-foot Sea Ray motor yacht, rocking and rolling. He could hear objects flying off the shelves down below. He imagined drawers opening and slamming closed and then cringed when he heard one extra loud crash he couldn't begin to identify.

As usual, God hadn't heard his prayer. The small houseboat in front of him nearly swamped, pitching hard from port to starboard and twisting violently in the gigantic wave. The captain was doing his best to keep her steady but not really succeeding.

"Typical," Cullen mumbled under his breath. "Thanks again, God."

Cullen heard the captain of the houseboat hail *Knot Nice*, the Cabo yacht, on the VHF radio, and he smiled when the captain called the guy every name under the sun.

Knot Nice *is right.* Cullen had half a mind to hail the Coast Guard and report the maniac but figured unless they witnessed him operating his vessel dangerously, they really wouldn't do anything but give him a warning.

When the danger passed and Cullen had made sure the tiny houseboat didn't need assistance, he put his boat in neutral, and breaking his own golden rule, he left the helm and ran down below. He never ever left the helm while underway, but since he'd decided to make this trip alone, he'd have to fudge on that rule a little.

He just needed a few seconds to make sure there were no real catastrophes belowdecks. The saloon was a mess, with things strewn everywhere, but nothing that couldn't wait until he docked later that afternoon. Cullen was about to head back to the helm when he spotted a pile of broken glass lying on the galley floor. Dread washed over him. *Cole's vase.* Cullen closed his eyes and dropped his head in defeat. Then suddenly he looked up to the heavens and slammed his fist down onto the companionway steps. "Seriously, God? Of all the things to break?"

Angry and forlorn, Cullen again took the helm, but his mood was now drastically different. So far, his trip from Provincetown, Massachusetts, to Southport, North Carolina, had gone exceptionally well. And if he were being honest, he had enjoyed it more than he'd anticipated, but now he was just ready for it to be over. And luckily for him, today was the last leg. Southport was just about a hundred miles ahead of him.

He radioed the bridge tender for the Wrightsville Beach drawbridge, made the next opening, and was now cruising along at eighteen knots in an uninhabited stretch of the waterway. He looked at his watch. *Six more hours, Cullen. You can do this.*

Diligently paying attention to the other snowbirds leaving the fast-approaching winter behind and making their way south for warmer climates, Cullen wondered about all the people onboard each boat he encountered. Who were they? What was their story? Where were they headed? For a quick moment, he questioned if they wondered the same about him. If they did, he'd bet his life they'd never guess his plight.

Occasionally someone would radio him, switch to another frequency, and chat about where *he* was going, along with their own plans, but almost everyone would compliment him on the name of his boat and his logo. *T-Time* had a unique logo—a T-shirt with a large *T* across the chest and the word *Time* next to it. It had been Cole's idea, and everyone thought it had to do with golf, but it was really an homage to Province T's, Cole's T-shirt shop in Provincetown.

Being on the water had its usual effect on Cullen. His mood slowly improved, and he was finally starting to enjoy the unusually mild late October day. It was hard not to. The skies were bright blue, the winds were mild, and the currents were in his favor. He was even filled with a little anticipation for what lay ahead for him.

After spending the last winter in P-town, enduring the endless blizzards and blistering cold and navigating four feet of snow on the ground all season, he'd decided he definitely wasn't doing that again. So he'd closed up the T-shirt shop on Columbus Day and headed south to spend the winter in North Carolina.

With just an hour to go before reaching his final destination, Cullen passed through Snow's Cut waterway, and when he made the turn into the Cape Fear River, he was instantly reminded of the movie by the same name. It involved a convicted rapist who spent fourteen years in prison but eventually got out on a technicality and went in search of the prosecutor who put him away. He began to stalk the prosecutor and his family, who fled to their houseboat docked on the Cape Fear River and…. He forced himself to think of something else. That movie had scared the crap out of him and Cole, and he didn't want to associate that fear or any negativity with his new winter home *or* with his memories of his and Cole's time in Southport.

On the long and very straight stretch of the Cape Fear River, Cullen engaged his autopilot and relaxed a little, recounting his trip. His journey had started at first light seven days ago. He'd crossed the Cape Cod Bay, watching the impending sunrise while sipping on his morning coffee. Eventually the cliffs and white sandy beaches of Cape Cod Bay gave way to the rocky shores of the Cape Cod Canal, which then took him through Buzzards Bay, Rhode Island Sound, and into Long Island Sound, where he spent his first night in Montauk, New York. The next few days brought him to the Atlantic Ocean and eventually to the entrance to the Intracoastal Waterway at Norfolk, Virginia. From there it was smooth sailing toward Southport.

His mind wandered from his journey to his destination. Why Southport, of all the places he could have chosen? His only rationale was that he and Cole had made this trip two years ago, and the

Southport Marina had been one of their stops on the way back up to Provincetown from Key West. While they were there, a production company had been filming the movie *Safe Haven*, with Julianne Hough and Josh Duhamel, and he and Cole had fallen in love with the charming little town.

On his and Cole's last day, they had stopped at a small wine and cheese shop near the marina and picked up a few bottles of wine, several cheeses, and a loaf of fresh-baked french bread. They'd sat on the bow of *T-Time* and watched the golden sun disappear below the horizon as they consumed their bounty. At about nine o'clock that evening, they were just about to turn in for the night when the crack of fireworks filled the night air and bright colors suddenly adorned the sky. The fireworks continued off and on for almost three hours. They'd found out from a dockhand when they were leaving that the movie crew had been filming a fireworks scene, and they had apparently needed multiple takes. It had been a magical evening, filled with wonder and amazement. Cullen remembered being as happy as he'd ever been. Little did he know that night had been the calm before the shit storm.

CHAPTER TWO

SHAKING OFF the memories, Cullen rounded the bend where the Cape Fear River ended and the Intracoastal Waterway resumed. To his portside was Bald Head Island and the inlet from the Atlantic Ocean, and directly ahead to starboard was the Southport Marina. The little town of Southport was finally in sight. He slowed to idle speed and radioed the marina for docking information.

The marina gave him his instructions, and he in turn informed them he was onboard alone and would need assistance at the dock. He put *T-Time* in neutral and once again left the helm to ready his lines. He wasn't sure if he was pleased or not when they directed him to the main dock and a slip directly across from the slip he and Cole had occupied on their previous trip.

It was nearing three thirty by the time Cullen connected the boat to the power supply, water, and cable television, and checked all the lines, making sure his boat was secure.

Cullen then ventured down below to clean up the mess left behind by the captain of *Knot Nice*. He grumbled under his breath as he put all the waterway guides, magazines, books, candles, and the pictures of him and Cole back in their proper places. Then he looked in the direction of the galley. In his shaking hand, he still held one of his favorite pictures of Cole, who was arranging tulips in a small crystal vase and smiling up at the camera. The remains of that vase now covered the galley floor, along with the half dozen red and yellow tulips that always filled the vase when Cullen was onboard.

Distraught, Cullen dropped to his knees to gather the flowers. He mentally cursed himself for not doing a better job of securing the vase that morning when he'd left Beaufort. But in a moment of anger, he shifted the blame. "No! I wedged it tightly behind the sink where it's made each leg of this trip unharmed." He once again looked up. "God! I'm getting really tired of these constant tests. You've already turned your back on me, so why can't you just leave me alone. When is all of this going to end?"

As he sifted through the broken glass, a shard tore at Cullen's index finger. "Damn!" Blood was now dripping onto the galley floor. "Are you seriously trying to push me over the edge?"

When he reached for a paper towel, Cullen knelt on another shard of glass. "Damn it!" he screamed. "Please! Just give me a break!"

Cullen fought the tears welling up in his eyes. In the last year and a half, he'd been so angry—at God and everyone else—he hadn't been able to cry. But no matter how determined he was to keep his emotions in check, on this day of all days, he lost the battle in a big way.

Today was the first of his planned attempt at leaving the past behind and finally moving on. But Cullen's tears had a mind of their own. They freely escaped the prison that had held them at bay for so long. Tear after tear ran down his cheeks, dripping like melting ice and mixing with the blood on the floor.

Emotionally exhausted, bleeding, and still majorly pissed off, Cullen sat back against the galley wall and gave in. His shoulders slumped forward in defeat and started to shake violently as he brought his hands up to cover his face. He cried. And cried. And cried.

How much time passed, he didn't know. But after his tears dried and he regained some semblance of stability, he got to his feet. He felt lighter somehow. His knee hurt and his heart still ached, but the pain seemed almost manageable for the first time in a long time.

He'd cried for Cole only once, and back then he'd been so lost and alone, no amount of tears could have lightened his load. But now, with over a year behind him and his memory of Cole fading.... *Wait! A thought hit him. Is this why I chose Southport? Not simply because we liked the town, but because I'm afraid Cole's memory is fading? Did I subconsciously want to be somewhere with a connection to him? But I'm supposed to be moving on. Shit!*

Confused, Cullen started cleaning up the mess by collecting what pieces of glass he could and placing them in a small cardboard box. He put the flowers in a cup with some water and swept up the rest of the particles.

"Good going, Cul," he said out loud. Cul was what Cole used to call him. "You weren't even here an hour before you lost it. Hey, but at least you figured out why you came here. Now to figure out if you should stay or not. This is supposed to be moving on. Remember?"

With no answers presenting themselves, Cullen decided to shower and get something to eat. After brushing his teeth, he studied his reflection in the mirror. His first thought was that he looked older somehow. His hair was still as black as coal, albeit with a little silver starting to appear at his temples. His crystal-blue eyes were still bright, and his Irish complexion was as fair as ever, but he looked older. *Maybe you just feel older, Cullen.*

On the way to the flybridge, Cullen stopped in the galley and opened a bottle of pinot noir. He poured himself a glass and climbed the steps. He took a sip of his wine and looked across the main dock to the slip *T-Time* had once occupied when he and Cole were here together. Cullen imagined his boat there again, Cole bending over and neatly flemishing all her lines—something Cullen always paid special attention to now because Cole loved the look so much. It always amazed him how the simple act of coiling a line like a rattlesnake gave Cole so much pleasure. Cullen heard Cole's voice in his head. *"She doesn't look properly docked if her lines aren't flemished."*

Cullen held his glass up in a toast to Cole. *You are no longer with me, my love, but I promise* T-Time's *lines will always be flemished.*

Then the realization hit him. *If I'm gonna try to move on with my life, I can't stay here. I need to let Cole go.*

It was all starting to make complete sense to him now. The fear of Cole's memory fading was why his subconscious had brought him back here. *Cullen! You stupid fool. It was all a way to try and hold on to him. Well, that settles it. I'll stay a couple of days, say good-bye for good, and move farther south. A place where there are no ties and no memories to hold on to.*

With his mind made up, Cullen downed his wine and went in search of a restaurant for dinner. He exited the marina and followed East Bay Street along the shoreline, taking the same route into town he and Cole had run each morning on their prior visit.

Stopping when he recognized the spot where the movie set—a little country store—had been constructed, Cullen stood and stared at the piece of vacant land at the water's edge. A great deal of the movie had taken place in the small fake storefront, and he imagined it still standing there with its fresh produce in baskets on the front porch.

In the last scene of the movie, the store had burned to the ground. He and Cole had stood on the sidelines with the other onlookers, watching the controlled flames fueled by propane canisters consuming the little structure. It had been bittersweet to watch the movie alone when it had finally been released.

Shaking off the memories, Cullen continued on. When he reached the waterfront, there were several options from which to choose. He decided on a little place called Fishy Fishy Cafe. It was nothing more than a hole in the wall, but Cullen had remembered having the best fish tacos of his life there, and he was hoping for a repeat performance. He seated himself at a small square table facing west, overlooking the waterway. He ordered a shot of Gentleman Jack, deciding to hold off on dinner for a little while. He had nowhere to go and was in no hurry. Besides, he had lots of memories to keep him company.

Cullen was in some sort of a trance when the last blurred edges of the sun dipped below the horizon, leaving behind only traces of an orange-and-fuchsia sky. He jumped when the waitress cleared her throat.

"Oh, sorry," she said. "I didn't mean to startle you."

Cullen smiled politely.

"Are you ready to order?"

Cullen cleared his throat. "Oh, sorry. Sure. Are the fish tacos still good?"

"The best," she said.

"Perfect. I'll have the fish tacos and, if you don't mind, a glass of pinot noir."

When the food came, Cullen looked down at the heaping dish of overstuffed fish tacos and crispy french fries. *Prepare yourself, Cullen. Nothing is ever really as good as you remember.*

But after the first bite, he had to concede. *I stand corrected. These* are *as good as I remembered.* And that finally brought a smile to his face.

Cullen ate in silence, his memories keeping him company. When he was finished, he paid his check and left the restaurant. He wasn't quite ready to turn in for the evening, so he decided a short walk was in order. He continued on his earlier route and ended up at the Historic Southport Riverwalk. That too was as charming as he'd remembered. *Two for two!*

Looking around, he noticed small white lights strung in all the massive oak trees and a gazebo in the center of the quaint little park. Inside the gazebo, a band was playing Carolina beach music, and people were either on their feet dancing or lying on picnic blankets enjoying the free show. Cullen took a seat on one of the many wooden swings dotting the sidewalk and listened.

In between songs he could hear the muffled voices of the adults and the laughter of the local kids running around the park. As the music started again, one little girl caught his attention. She squealed with delight as a man he assumed was her father picked her up, swung her around, and held her in his arms as he carried her onto the dance floor.

With a smile on his face, Cullen watched the little girl and her dad dance playfully until the song ended. She wrapped her little arms around the man's neck and hugged him tightly as he took her back to their blanket and put her down next to a very pregnant lady.

He, of course, couldn't hear what she was saying, but her little mouth was moving a mile a minute, and her mother was smiling broadly. The man sat down next to them, took the pregnant woman's hand in his, and kissed it. He smiled at the little girl again, kissed her on the cheek, and lay back on his elbows and looked up at the stars. He pointed at the dark sky with one finger and said something to the little girl. She looked up and followed to where he was pointing. She said something else, and he moved his finger to another position as she smiled in wonderment.

Cullen watched the three of them for the longest time. When the band finally stopped, the man helped the pregnant woman to her feet, folded their blanket, and threw it over his shoulder. He scooped the little girl into his arms, and Cullen watched, still smiling, as the family walked away. For a second it actually warmed his heart to think God had blessed some people with pure love and happiness. And then his heart turned cold. *But not me.*

Somewhere along the line, Cullen had decided that God had turned his back on him. God had taken away everything that had mattered to him, and now he was left to navigate his empty life. Alone. He stood, stuck his hands in his pockets, and walked back to his boat.

CHAPTER THREE

MOSTLY OUT of habit, Cullen was awake and staring at the porthole in his cabin as the break of dawn breached the small oval window. He rolled onto his back and stretched. Unfortunately, he woke as tired as when he'd gone to bed. He sat up, swung his feet around, planted them firmly on the floor, and looked at the clock: 6:18.

He rubbed his tired eyes, yawned, and stretched again, half wanting to crawl back into bed and pull the covers up over his head. It had been a restless night. Cullen had been plagued with disturbing dreams, none of which he could remember at the moment. They hadn't been nightmares per se, and they were teetering on the edge of his memory, but he just couldn't recall them. *A run will help clear my head.*

Cullen dressed and stretched his muscles. He stuck his earbuds in. Usually he listened to either NPR or some type of music while he ran, but today he needed to think. He wanted to clear his head so he could remember his dreams, and the morning news or lively music might interfere. So the only thing he heard in his earbuds today was the cell phone application that calculated his distance, as well as the calories he'd burned.

"Start your workout," the app ordered.

Cullen ran down the dock, passed the marina office, and followed mostly the same route he'd taken last night. But instead of going past the restaurant, he took a left on Brunswick Street through a nice neighborhood that bordered the waterfront. He turned right on Caswell, and if he remembered correctly, Caswell eventually ran into the Riverwalk. Then he could take North Howe back to W. West Street and eventually to the marina.

As usual once he got into his groove, Cullen's head started to clear. He remembered that his dreams had had something to do with Cole and Southport, but that's as far as he got.

His thoughts were interrupted by a British woman's voice in his ear. "Time: twenty-seven minutes and thirty-two seconds. Distance:

three miles. Current pace: nine minutes thirty-two seconds. Average pace: nine minutes fifty-five seconds. Split pace: ten minutes and three seconds per mile."

Wow! Three miles already. The time had flown by, and he was just turning onto the sidewalk of the Riverwalk. He looked at his watch. It was nearing seven o'clock, but the park was pretty much deserted except for one man in the distance, sitting on a park bench with a book in his hand. The closer Cullen got to the park bench, the more detail he could see. It was not just a man, but a very handsome man. Strawberry blond. Almost a ginger. Close-cut beard. Probably blue or green eyes and very nicely dressed in a shirt and tie. Cullen was suddenly intrigued. But something was off. The guy's elbows rested on his knees, and his shoulders were hunched over in sort of a defeated position. He was rubbing the top of his book and gazing out over the water. As Cullen approached he could see the man's expression, and it was one of obvious desperation, or at the very least, deep sadness.

The sun was now above the horizon and well on its way to brightening the early morning sky when the guy just happened to move his book a certain way. It caught one of the sun's rays, sending a reflection right into Cullen's eyes. In that moment, Cullen knew the man's book wasn't just any old book. It was the Bible, and the sun was reflecting off of the gilded edges of the pages.

Cullen slowed his pace to a jog. He watched as the guy gazed out onto the open water and rubbed the top of his Bible, an expression of sadness and defeat on his face. *He reeks of desperation.* Cullen's formal training took over with no conscious thought on his part, and he was suddenly contemplating his options. *Stop and see if he needs anything? See if I can provide assistance? Offer to call a friend or family member?*

No, Cullen! Stop! This is no longer my line of work or my problem. I run a T-shirt shop now. Just keep the hell going.

But something was nagging at Cullen. He felt an odd kinship to this man. A total stranger, yes, but it was a feeling he couldn't shake. He kept a close watch on the guy, who seemed oblivious to anything or anyone except his own thoughts. As Cullen approached the man, he told himself to keep on jogging.

There are at least ten other empty benches, not to mention all the swings. If you stop and sit on his bench, it's gonna look very suspicious.

He's gonna think you're trying to pick him up or something. Just keep going, Cullen!

Cullen was within feet of the park bench and still undecided whether to stop or run like hell. He silently begged his legs to keep going, but it was no use. The damn things had a mind of their own and stopped right in front of the bench. As if that weren't enough, his sweaty ass helped itself to the empty seat just inches from the guy.

Breathing heavily and not knowing what else to do, Cullen put his head down between his legs. He turned his head a little so he would be ready if the guy decided to hit him or something, but to his relief, no fist came in his direction. Still the guy immediately slid over to the opposite edge of the bench, looking genuinely startled. He eyed Cullen nervously, like he thought maybe Cullen was going to rob him.

Cullen spoke. "Sorry, I needed to sit for a second."

The guy's expression then morphed into one of concern. "You… you okay, man?"

Relief washed over Cullen. "Just a little light-headed," he lied. "I guess I've been pushing it a little too hard."

"Do you need me to call 911 or something?"

"No, no. I just need a few minutes to catch my breath." Cullen sat up again and looked at the man's Bible. "I'm really sorry if I'm interrupting your prayer time. I didn't mean to intrude."

The guy followed Cullen's gaze down to the book in his hand and then looked up again, seeming confused. When their eyes met, Cullen held the man's gaze. *Yep! They're green all right. The deepest damn emerald green eyes I've ever seen. And his eyelashes….* They were long and a deep red with golden tips. In the bright sunlight, he resembled some sort of angel.

"Oh!" the guy said, apparently getting Cullen's reference to the Bible. He looked back out over the water again and sighed. "Don't worry," he said sarcastically. "He's not listening anyway."

Cullen's affinity to this stranger strengthened. *I know how you feel, man!* Without thinking he stuck his hand out. "I'm Cullen Kiley."

The guy eyed Cullen suspiciously and stared at his outstretched hand.

Cullen pulled his hand back. "I'm sorry. I don't usually introduce myself to strangers. But to be totally honest, I'm not really winded. I noticed you sitting here, and… well, you just looked like you needed a friend. Like you were struggling with some big life decision or something. I just wanted to make sure you're okay."

The guy's facial features softened some, but he didn't respond. He turned and looked back out over the water, the same sad expression once again consuming his face.

"But… I—I was afraid if I stopped you might think I was trying to rob you or, even worse, come on to you."

The guy snapped his head back in Cullen's direction, and his eyes appeared to darken to an even deeper shade of green. "Are you?" he asked hesitantly.

Cullen laughed. "No! I was just running by, and… well, I've been trained to pick up on certain signs, and sometimes a person's body language and ah…. As I said, you looked like you could use a friend."

"Trained to pick up on certain signs or a person's body language?" the man repeated.

Cullen looked down at the ground, wishing he'd chosen his words more carefully. "Yeah. It's a long story."

This time the guy stuck out his hand. "I'm Abel Weston."

The two men shook. "Nice to meet you, Abel. So… are you okay?"

Abel seemed to be thinking over the question. "A little lost. At a crossroads, maybe. And feeling forgotten and left behind, but other than that, I'm just dandy."

Abel was quiet for a long time, and Cullen afforded him the time he needed to gather his thoughts. After several minutes passed, Abel spoke again, his voice low and unsure.

"Do you ever wonder why God answers prayers for some and not others?"

Shit! Cullen had no idea how he was going to reply to that one. He sure as hell didn't have any answers when it came to God or unanswered prayers. He and the man upstairs had gone their separate ways over a year ago. "Look, Abel, I'm probably not the best guy to talk to about God. He and I are not on the best of terms these days."

"You too, huh?" Abel looked at his Bible. "The problem for me is, well, God is my job. And it's damn hard to preach about or counsel people on God's love and his plan when you don't feel it yourself."

God is his job? "Are you a member of the clergy?" Cullen was pretty sure he already knew the answer.

"Associate pastor." Abel held up his Bible and nodded over his shoulder. "Southport Baptist Church. Just up the street there."

Cullen nodded. "You look awful young to be an associate pastor."

"I get that a lot." Abel chuckled. "But I'm thirty-five. Just look younger, I guess."

Cullen nodded and then another long silence ensued.

"Southport is a small town," Abel finally said. "Haven't seen you around before."

"I just got here yesterday. I'm staying on my boat over at the Southport Marina."

"Oh. I live just a few blocks from there."

More silence until Abel broke it.

"Well… if you're hanging around for a while, maybe you can come to Sunday service, and we can see about at least trying to mend *your* relationship with the Almighty."

Cullen almost snorted. "I appreciate the offer and the effort, but you can take your pastor hat off when you're talking to me. My relationship with God is… well, let's just say over. With little chance of reconciliation."

Abel frowned. "I'm sorry. I don't know why I said that. Habit, I guess. But I sort of know what you mean. It's so difficult going to work every day, playing the part of an associate pastor and continuously doubting my calling. So when I can't take it anymore, I come out here and just sit. It sort of renews me. For a little while anyway."

They were both now looking out over the water, as if it held all the answers somewhere just under the surface.

"How long are you staying?" Abel asked awkwardly.

"Originally for the winter, but… my plans have changed."

Abel nodded this time. "That's too bad. You would like Southport. Small and sleepy but charming at the same time. I've been here about a year now, and it has really grown on me."

"Yeah?" Another long silence hung in the air. Cullen cleared his throat. "Look, man. If you wanna talk about what's on your mind, I'm a pretty good listener."

Abel shook his head. "It's no use. Nothing you or anyone else can do for me. I'm in this one alone."

Wanting to leave the man with his dignity and avoid prying, Cullen stood. "Okay, then. As long as you're okay, I guess I'll be on my way."

Abel stood too. Cullen quickly looked the man over.

Abel was a few inches shorter then Cullen's own six-foot-two-inch frame, and he appeared to be very fit. Gym-like fit. With broad shoulders and a small waist. The sun was reflecting off of his boyish reddish-blond locks, and his green eyes sparkled in the sun's reflection off the water.

Apparently back in pastor mode, Abel flashed a smile, and Cullen swallowed a gasp. Abel's entire face lit up. "Thanks for stopping. It was very kind and considerate of you."

What a smile. If this is what he looks like while he's carrying the weight of the world on his shoulders, he must light up the universe when he's carefree.

Cullen cleared his throat. "No problem. Take care of yourself, Abel."

Cullen turned to leave.

"Cullen?" Abel asked.

Cullen stopped and looked back at Abel.

"Are you by any chance a member of the clergy yourself?"

Shit! Good going, Cullen. Now how are you gonna get out of this one? You can't lie to the guy.

Cullen sighed and accepted his fate. "Used to be. But it now seems like a lifetime ago. How could you tell?"

Abel smiled again, and Cullen felt a pang of something unidentifiable deep inside of him. "Oh, I don't know. Maybe your mannerisms. Your compassion for your fellow man. The way your voice reassures a person everything is gonna be okay. And… the fact that you said you were trained for this sort of thing. Separately these things mean nothing, but put them all together and you get a man of the cloth."

Cullen was sincerely impressed. *The man is a listener all right. Even when the person he's listening to isn't saying anything.*

"The only thing I can't pinpoint is which religion."

Cullen chuckled. "I'm a retired Episcopal priest."

"Damn." Abel smiled, and then he blushed. "If I were a betting man—and for the record, I'm not—I would have gone with Methodist."

Cullen found himself a little thrown off balance. He hadn't talked about his past in quite a while. He knew he was bouncing nervously from one foot to the other, but he couldn't help it. "Well, I think I need to let you get back to your one-on-one time with the big guy."

Abel looked a little disappointed, but if he was, he didn't voice it. He just held out his hand again. "You be safe and happy, Cullen Kiley. Wherever your path takes you."

Cullen shook Abel's hand and then impulsively laid his other hand over Abel's heart. "And remember. Whatever you're praying for, I know if you look deep enough in here, you'll find all the right answers."

Abel reached up and placed his hand over Cullen's. "Thank you."

Warmth ran through Cullen, and for a moment he felt almost alive—a feeling he hadn't experienced in a very long time.

Abel lowered his hand, and a smile graced his lips. Cullen smiled as well. Something had passed between them just then. Something odd but also comforting.

"Take care." Cullen took off running and didn't stop. He had no idea what was propelling him or what he was running from, but by the time he got back to the boat, the lady in his phone said he'd run nearly eight miles. He sat in the cockpit totally exhausted and stared down at the sun shimmering on the water. Out of the blue, memories of his dream started coming back to him. In little pieces, at first, and then as one came to him, so did others.

It was a heavenly day. The sun was high in the bright blue sky, and the seas were calm. He and Cole were aboard T-Time, *cruising the Atlantic Ocean. For some odd reason, Cole had gone down to the swim platform, and after a few minutes, he hadn't returned. Cullen stopped the boat and went to check on him, and he was not there. Cullen ran below, calling Cole's name frantically. But no one answered. Cullen looked out over the water, and in the distance he saw Cole fighting to stay afloat but drifting farther and farther away.*

Cullen ran down to the swim platform, but Cole was too far away to toss him a life ring. With no other options, Cullen jumped in to save him. No matter how fast or far Cullen swam, Cole was always just out of reach, waving his hands and calling Cullen's name.

Cullen turned to look for the boat, which was nowhere in sight. When he turned back, Cole was also gone. Cullen scanned the surface in every direction. Nothing. He frantically called Cole's name, but no response came. After panicking and flailing in the water for who knows how long, Cullen was suddenly overcome with exhaustion. His arms and legs would no longer move, and he finally decided to give up. He cursed God, raised his arms into the air, and sank peacefully beneath the surface. As he calmly descended into the abyss, he cocked his head and watched the sun's rays shimmer under the surface. He began to inwardly gasp for oxygen, but of course there was none. His body bucked and heaved for the nonexistent air. When he could no longer hold his breath, Cullen closed his eyes and opened his mouth, inhaling as much salty seawater as he could get into his lungs. His body convulsed once, maybe twice, and then it was over.

Damn, Cullen! He wrapped his arms around himself and rubbed his forearms, suddenly bitterly cold.

Cullen shook his head, trying to shake the dream he'd worked so hard to remember. His thoughts quickly drifted to another person he thought was also drowning: Abel. Something was definitely weighing heavily on the man's mind and bringing him down, but what? Abel hadn't given him any clue, and it had set his mind wondering.

Cullen showered and sat on the edge of his bed. He cradled his head in his hands, suddenly emotionally drained and physically exhausted. He couldn't escape his feelings of inadequacy for not being able to save Cole in his dream, or his helplessness in regard to Abel.

Cullen pulled back the covers and climbed into bed. His last thought before he drifted off was of the ginger-headed stranger.

WHEN CULLEN woke he was very disoriented. He sat up, trying to determine his whereabouts, but the room was pitch black except for the red glow of the numbers on a digital clock: 7:32. He instinctively felt for a lamp next to the bed and flipped the switch. *The boat. You're on* T-Time.

Cullen glanced at the clock again. *Jeez, Cullen. It's 7:35. In the evening? You slept all damn day? And into the night?* He pulled back the covers, swung his bare feet around, and planted them on the teak and ivory floor. He was hungry and thirsty, but above all he had to pee.

After taking care of business, Cullen drank what seemed like a gallon of water and then showered and dressed in khakis and a baby blue golf shirt. He started walking out of the marina with dinner on his mind and remembered a little restaurant he and Cole had enjoyed on North Howe Street called Ports of Call, which was owned by a gay couple. If memory served, Cullen remembered how to get there. And truth be told, he was well rested and had nothing better to do, so why not walk? It was only eight blocks or so, and it was a very nice night.

Cullen strolled four blocks up W. West Street to North Howe and turned right. He stopped dead in his tracks when he looked across the street and saw the Southport Baptist Church. *Abel's church.*

The stately red brick building with its single white steeple, bell tower, and small chapel off to the right consumed the entire block. It was not at all what he'd expected. Not that he'd actually pictured it in his mind, but if he had, this wasn't it.

As he studied the building, he decided it was far less formal than an Episcopal, Presbyterian, or Catholic church, but statelier than the many small Baptist churches that lined Cape Cod. Somehow it reminded him of a small country church one might see at the head of a valley somewhere in the mountains. It was larger, of course, but was charming in its own way. It fit its surroundings perfectly, and that made Cullen smile.

Some type of gathering had just ended, and people were exiting the church, milling about and standing on the steps conversing. He quickly scanned the crowd, looking for any sign of Abel speaking to or saying good night to his congregation, but no such luck. He had no idea what he would have done had he seen Abel, but luckily he didn't have to make that decision.

Cullen hesitantly started walking again, still scanning the crowd until he crossed the street onto the next block. *Let's see. If the restaurant is still in business, it will be up ahead on the right in a block or two.* When he entered the next block, he smiled as he recognized the red brick building with the blue-and-white awnings. *Whataya know? It's still here.*

Stepping inside, Cullen realized the restaurant was crowded but not full to capacity. Off to the right, behind the bar was a guy playing guitar and singing a James Taylor song. Cullen listened for a moment and smiled when he recognized the song as "Sweet Baby James." It had been one of Cole's favorites.

Am I ever going to go someplace or do something that doesn't remind me of Cole? For the first time, he realized the answer to that question was a big fat no. *But isn't that why you're here? To not forget?* When his family and friends convinced him it was time to at least make an attempt to move on with his life, they probably never imagined he would end up here.

Cullen nodded his head along to the music, enjoying the soothing waltz-like melody. He listened intently until a guy he recognized as one of the owners approached him. "Mike's great, isn't he?"

"He is. That song brings back so many memories."

The owner smiled but thankfully didn't ask him to elaborate. "Going solo tonight?"

"I'm afraid so." Cullen didn't take the time to reintroduce himself. He didn't have the heart to explain for the thousandth time where Cole was. He didn't want the pity. Not tonight.

"Right this way, then." The owner started walking across the restaurant, and Cullen followed. On the way, Cullen stopped, dug into his billfold, pulled out a twenty, and smiled as he put it in the tip bowl on the stool next to Mike. Mike nodded and smiled back but kept on singing. Cullen was shown to a table for two, and after he sat, the owner removed one of the place settings and quickly disappeared.

The evening was a pleasant one, devoid of any meltdowns or anger brought on by painful memories, and Cullen was enjoying himself immensely. Halfway through his meal, Mike took a break and stopped by to thank Cullen for the tip. Up close he was a handsome man with shaggy brown hair and eyes the color of caramel that, if used as a superpower, could have easily melted a person who stared too long. When they shook hands, Mike held on to Cullen's hand a little longer than protocol demanded, smiled warmly, and winked. He was soft-spoken and gazed into Cullen's eyes intensely as he laid a business card on the table.

Mike lingered a little longer and then nodded. "Have a great evening."

"You too," Cullen said.

Maybe I still have it. Cullen wasn't interested, of course. He'd not been with anyone since Cole, but it sure felt nice to know someone still found him attractive.

After an exceptional dinner, a little healthy reminiscing about his and Cole's time here, and Mike's smooth voice—and moves—it was finally time to call it a night. He paid the check and made his way to the door. When he passed Mike, the singer waved and winked again.

Cullen could have sworn Mike mouthed the words "call me," but he couldn't be sure. Cullen stepped out into the chill of the fall night and inhaled the crisp salty air.

He'd slept the entire day and wasn't quite ready to go back to the boat, so he exited the restaurant and headed for the Riverwalk. When he hit the water's edge, he turned left and entered the park where he and Abel had had their encounter.

He strolled along the sidewalk, feeling all right for the first time in a very long time. Cullen stopped at one of the swings and took a seat. The hinges creaked and whined as he moved the wooden porch swing back and forth, but the sound was more soothing than annoying, reminding him of the porch swing at his grandparents' farm in upstate New York.

He and his brother, as well as his cousins, had spent many summers there when they were all kids, and they ended every day with family time on the porch, either swinging or rocking, after dinner. He hadn't thought about that place in years. His grandparents and the farm were now long gone, but he suddenly realized he still had the memories. Sure, something had to jog them, but they were still there, like it had all happened yesterday.

The answer descended on him like a ton of bricks. It would be the same way with his memories of Cole. Wouldn't it? Cullen's fear of forgetting Cole scared him almost as much as losing the man himself. Their memories together were really all he had left to hold on to.

You won't *lose them, Cullen. Just like all your other memories, they may fade a little over time, but just like this stupid old porch swing did, something—a smell, a sound, a song, a photograph—will always bring them flooding back.*

Cullen looked up, taken aback when he heard a soft voice. "I didn't mean to startle you, but this time you look like *you* could use a friend."

Surprised, Cullen grinned. "Abel?" The handsome face looking down at him was stoic but laced with genuine concern.

"Are you okay?"

Cullen thought for a moment. "Yeah. I'm working on it, but for now I am."

Abel looked at the empty spot on the swing and then back up to Cullen.

Cullen jumped to his feet. "Where are my manners? Please, will you join me?"

For some odd reason, Cullen was suddenly concerned for his new friend. Abel's expression was much like what he had worn earlier in the day. They both sat, and Cullen rested his hands on his lap and looked out over the water. "I might be okay right now, but I don't think you are."

Silence lingered between them for a moment, and then Abel stretched out and rested his arm on the back of the bench. "It was a really tough night."

"You wanna talk about it?"

Abel continued to stare out over the darkness of the Cape Fear River. "It would do no good."

Swinging together in the darkness of the crisp fall night in perfect rhythm, the screech and whine of the swing protesting every move, Cullen counted the seconds between each time the Oak Island Lighthouse far off in the distance bathed them in the glow of its lamp.

In one of the rotations, Cullen could have sworn he saw the light reflect off of a single tear sliding down Abel's cheek. Unable to let it go, Cullen finally said, "It might."

"It was just another Bible study with those holier-than-thou, Southern Baptist, backwoods attitudes. I don't think the church will ever change."

"So that's what was going on," Cullen said. "I passed by the church on my way to dinner and saw the crowd mingling on the steps."

"I thought that was you," Abel said. "I waved, but you were already gone. I had some things to do in the church, but as soon as I finished, I took a chance and walked over. I was hoping I'd find you here."

Cullen looked back out over the water. "What verses of the Bible were you studying tonight?"

More silence. And then Abel sighed. It seemed like he was about to finally take Cullen into his confidence. But instead, they both jumped at the sound of a woman's voice.

"Pastor Weston?"

Abel jumped to his feet. "Courtney! Hey. What are you doing here?"

Cullen listened as the girl explained. "I saw you walk this way after Bible study, so I followed you. I just wanted to tell you that you did a great job tonight with those old coots."

Courtney looked between Abel and Cullen. "Oh. Courtney. This is uh... uh... Reverend Cullen Kiley. He's an Episcopal priest visiting Southport for a few days."

What the...? Episcopal priest?

Cullen stood and extended his hand. "Uh... that's retired Episcopal priest. It's nice to meet you, Courtney."

Courtney shook Cullen's hand and looked back at Abel. "I didn't mean to interrupt, Pastor Weston. I just wanted you to know there are people in your corner. I'll let you gentlemen get back to your conversation."

"Oh no, Courtney. It's okay. It's too late to walk alone. Where are you parked?"

"Back at the church."

"Okay, then. I'll escort you."

Abel turned to Cullen and nervously extended his hand. "Good night, Reverend Kiley. It was great to see you. I hope I'll see you again before you leave." Abel's face was full of pain and misery, and it broke Cullen's heart.

"Good night, Pastor Weston."

Abel offered his arm to Courtney and led her back in the direction of the church. Cullen watched until they turned the corner and he could no longer see them. He sat back down on the swing and looked out over the water.

What the heck just happened? That was the most bizarre thing I think I've ever experienced. And where did that Reverend Kiley crap come from?

IT WAS almost midnight before Cullen climbed back onto *T-Time*. After Abel's swift departure, Cullen had spent over an hour sitting alone on the swing, hypnotized by the rotating glow of the Oak Island light and the sounds of the waves crashing against the seawall. As he pushed himself back and forth with one foot, the screeching and whining of the wooden swing lulled him into a rhythm. He contemplated his departure, and just before he left the park, he made a mental note that if he ever did come back to Southport, he should bring a can of WD-40 with him.

Now safely back onboard his boat, Cullen poured himself a couple of fingers of bourbon and settled topside to enjoy the clear, brisk evening. After much deliberation and weighing of the odds, Cullen decided he would get up at first light, run his five miles, and then cast off. Maybe Charleston and then maybe even farther south. The fun was in not knowing.

Run your five miles, huh? Yeah, right! You know you're hoping for one last chance meeting with Abel.

"So what if I am," Cullen said aloud and then looked around to make sure no one was in earshot as he talked to himself.

After panicking about forgetting Cole and the life they shared, followed by the almost juvenile revelation that he would never forget the man he'd loved or their life together, there was really no reason to hold on to the things they'd enjoyed together or the places they had visited. Therefore, there was nothing keeping him here.

Or was there? Something was nagging at him. Or someone, to be exact. Abel. He couldn't deny he was worried Abel was alone and wasn't going to make it through this tough time. Could he help the man in some way before he left?

Come on! You don't even know the guy. You met him on a random park bench, and he hasn't opened up to you, so how can you help him?

Their meeting had been a chance one. They had simply been two strangers who crossed paths in the early morning hours. One person reaching out to another person in a moment of distress. That's all. End of story.

Then why are you so hell-bent on helping the guy? And don't say you're doing this out of habit. You're retired and no longer required to do this kind of work. He doesn't need saving, and he's not one of your congregation. You no longer have a congregation.

That realization made Cullen think about his own situation for a moment. *How could you go from a happily married Episcopal priest with your own church and thriving congregation to where you are today?* Cullen looked up to the stars. *Shit happens! That's how!*

But Abel. He seems to be in so much pain. I can't just leave him. Sure you can! He's not your responsibility.

Logically Cullen knew all this debating and back and forth was stupid, but his head and his heart were two totally different things.

CHAPTER FOUR

CULLEN WOKE before the alarm sounded. There were no signs of light peeking through his cabin portholes, so he knew it was still fairly early. Rolling onto his back, he stretched and looked up at the ceiling, trying to gauge how he felt emotionally. He'd slept pretty well and hadn't been plagued by any bad dreams. *That's a start.*

Cullen glanced at the clock: 5:55. Without a second thought, he hopped out of bed, made a brief stop in the head, and ended up in the galley making coffee. While he waited for the coffee to brew, Cullen's thoughts drifted back to last night's internal tug of war. *Do I go, or do I stay?* He'd gone over every pro and con, and after much internal deliberation, just before he'd drifted off, he'd made the decision that when he went out for his run, if Abel was in the park, he would try one last time to get him to open up. If he didn't or wouldn't, Cullen would simply go. In truth he was still feeling pretty good about his game plan. "If I'm meant to stay it will work out that way," Cullen whispered while he poured his coffee.

Well! Listen to you, Cullen Kiley. Is that a little faith I hear in your voice?

"Absolutely not!" he mumbled and put the thought right out of his head.

Cullen sipped on his second cup of coffee and watched the bright orange-and-gold hues of a beautiful dawn filling the eastern sky. When he saw the arc of the sun peek over the horizon, he downed the rest of his coffee, went down below, and changed into his running clothes.

It was still a little chilly when Cullen stepped off the boat, and he was thankful he'd worn a long-sleeved running shirt. He started his exercise application, attached his cell phone to his right bicep, put his earbuds in, stretched, and took off down the dock. *Well, Kiley. Let's get a move on and see what the day brings.*

Cullen exited the marina at a brisk pace. He turned right on East Bay and ran along the front of the Municipal Marina. He figured taking a longer route would give Abel a little extra time to get to the Riverwalk—if indeed he was planning to go there. And if Abel happened to be there and they started talking, it would most likely be the stopping point for Cullen, so he wanted to get as much of a run in as possible before he reached the park.

After a half mile, Cullen turned left on Caswell and enjoyed the charming little neighborhood of clapboard houses painted in various pastel colors, all with white scroll work and lattice trim. After three more miles, he turned right onto South Atlantic Avenue and started working his way down to the Riverwalk. As soon as he rounded the corner, he could see the water off in the distance, and his heart started beating faster in anticipation of what he would find when he got there.

When Cullen was about a half mile from the water's edge, he started his sprint. He was tired of the building anticipation, and it was time to know if Abel was there or not. He pushed himself as hard as he could and sprinted across East Bay and into the park. He took to the sidewalk and almost stopped dead in his tracks when he rounded the turn and saw a guy sitting on one of the park benches. From the guy's body language and the sun reflecting off of his reddish-blond hair, Cullen could tell it was Abel. By the time he got there, his heart was nearly leaping out of his chest, and he was having a hard time breathing.

"Hey," Abel said, handing him a cup of coffee.

Cullen waved him off and dropped down next to him. He lowered his head between his legs and tried to catch his breath.

Abel laughed. "You don't have to fake fatigue this time."

"Not… faking." Cullen gasped for air. "Sprinted… the last… half mile."

Abel stood and put the two cups of coffee on the sidewalk. "Do I really need to call 911 this time?"

Cullen waved his hand in the air. "I'll be fine. Just give me a minute." No matter how out of breath Cullen was, he didn't miss how great Abel looked. He appeared to be very comfortable in a dark green V-neck sweater that really brought out the color in his eyes, blue jeans, and brown leather driving shoes with no socks. He'd been handsome in his suit, of course, but this was a different kind of handsome. More relaxed and youthful.

"If you say so." Abel sat back down and picked up his coffee cup.

Cullen stood and paced back and forth on the sidewalk. Three minutes passed before he started to regain some sort of even breathing. When Cullen looked up, Abel was smiling and sipping his coffee.

"What's so funny?"

"You."

"Me?"

"Yeah! Why do you torture yourself like that?"

"Oh, please," Cullen smirked. "I do it to try and compete with age and gravity. Why do *you* do it?"

Abel chuckled and once again offered Cullen the second cup of coffee. "I don't."

"You apparently do something. You're in great shape." Cullen accepted the cup.

"Thanks. The gym is my poison. Most days, at least an hour. Maybe two."

"Well, it shows." Cullen held up his coffee cup. "By the way, what's this?"

"A peace offering, I guess." Abel paused. "I really hoped I'd see you again before you left so I could apologize for being an ass last night."

Cullen sat next to Abel on the bench and nodded. "Yeah? What was that reverend crap all about? You know very well I'm retired and on not so good terms with the man upstairs."

Abel turned and looked Cullen in the eyes. "I'm really sorry. It was just an attack of paranoia."

Cullen tilted his head. "Paranoia? I don't understand."

Abel hesitated.

Here we go again. "Look, Abel. My plan is to leave Southport this morning. I came by here for one last opportunity to see if I could help you in some way before I left. But if I have any chance, you'll have to open up to me. If you don't feel comfortable enough to do that, then I'll be on my way. It's that simple." Cullen looked away. "I have my own demons to fight, ya know?"

"Please, don't go." Abel said it so low Cullen almost didn't hear him.

"Abel." Cullen sighed.

Abel took another sip of his coffee.

Cullen did the same and waited patiently.

"Last night at Bible study...." Abel's voice trailed off, and he cleared his throat. "We were debating homosexuality and the Bible. Pastor Williams argued against it, of course, and I was appointed to argue on its behalf. And by the end of the night, he had a bunch of the attendees about to get pitchforks, light torches, and drive the bad homosexuals out of town."

Cullen chuckled as the scene unfolded in his head.

But Abel stood and started pacing in front of the park bench. "Leviticus 18:22. 'You shall not lie with a male as with a woman. It is an abomination.' And 1 Corinthians 6:9–10. 'Do you not know that the unrighteous will not inherit the kingdom of God? Do not be deceived. Neither fornicators, nor idolaters, nor adulterers, nor homosexuals, nor sodomites, nor thieves, nor covetous, nor drunkards, nor revilers, nor extortioners will inherit the kingdom of God.

"These were just a couple of the verses he used. Can you believe the Bible lumps homosexuals in with thieves, adulterers, prostitutes, and alcoholics? Not to mention slanderers and swindlers. And don't get me started on what they said about Sodom and Gomorrah. Do you know the formal statement on homosexuality from the Southern Baptist Convention?"

"I don't," Cullen said.

"I do. Because I was forced to memorize it. 'We affirm God's plan for marriage and sexual intimacy—one man, and one woman, for life. Homosexuality is not a "valid alternative lifestyle." The Bible condemns it as sin. It is not, however, unforgivable sin. The same redemption available to all sinners is available to homosexuals. They, too, may become new creations in Christ.'"

"Sit, Abel." Cullen stood and took Abel by the shoulders. "In the story of Sodom and Gomorrah, God sent a couple of angels disguised as men to Sodom, where the men of Sodom threatened to gang rape them. The angels blinded the men, and then God destroyed the city. Abel, for centuries this story has been interpreted as God's judgment on homosexuality. But gang rape was the only form of same-sex behavior that was threatened."

Abel sat with an expression of surprise on his face.

"Furthermore," Cullen continued. "The recap of the story found in Ezekial 16:49 highlights what I believe is the *real* point of the story. 'Look, this was the iniquity of your sister Sodom: She and her daughter had pride, fullness of food, and abundance of idleness; neither did she strengthen the hand of the poor and needy.' So in other words, everyone using this story as evidence of the sin of homosexuality, in my opinion, is missing the point entirely."

Cullen sat down again and looked at Abel.

When their eyes met, Abel said, "Wow, I sure wish I'd had you with me last night."

"Come on, Abel. You know as well as I do the Bible contradicts itself over and over. For every verse that can be used against homosexuality, there are two verses that dispute that claim or contradict the original verse. Anyone arguing on behalf of or against anything can find all the ammunition they need, all in one place. And in my opinion," Cullen said, "God wrote the Bible to be an all-inclusive Word that can be interpreted in many different ways. The only problem with that is everyone seems to interpret it to suit their immediate needs."

"But can't they say the same about homosexuals?"

Touché! A reluctant smiled tugged at the corner of Cullen's mouth. "Sure they can." Cullen looked out over the water and blinked against the sun reflecting off of the rippling waves. "Two years ago I would have told you that *my* God loves everyone. He made us all the way we are, and no one has the right to judge anyone else for who they are or who they choose to love."

"And now?" Abel asked.

Cullen stared at a sailboat idling along the river, fighting the current, its large white sails luffing in the light breeze. "I still believe God made us who we are, and I also still believe that none of us have a right to judge another."

Abel sighed. "But you no longer believe that *your* God loves everyone?"

"No. I guess not." Cullen looked down into his lap. "But"—he looked at Abel and held up his index finger—"not because of their sexuality or who they love."

"Why, then?" Abel asked.

"I don't know why. I told you the first day we met that I wasn't the best guy to talk to about God. All I know is he seems to have turned his back on me."

Abel opened his mouth to speak, but Cullen put up a hand to stop him. "But what does all this have to do with you introducing me to that girl as Reverend Kiley last night and then tearing out of here like you weren't able to get away from me quick enough?"

"Like I said earlier. Pure paranoia."

"Elaborate," Cullen ordered.

It appeared Abel was trying to find the right words, so Cullen gave him a minute.

At last Abel spoke. "Well, I'd just spent two hours debating homosexuality, and I'd gotten some pretty angry comments, not to mention the mean and spiteful looks I was getting from a lot of the congregation. And to top it all off, hardly anyone spoke to me after the debate, and I started to think they were somehow seeing me differently. When Courtney followed me and saw the two of us sitting side by side, on a park bench, in the dark, my arm over the back of the bench, I panicked. I didn't know what she thought or what it looked like to her. But I thought if I introduced you as a reverend, that might squash any suspicions she might have had."

"Suspicions?" Cullen asked in an attempt to get Abel to actually say the words. "Suspicions of what?"

Abel hesitated again.

"Come on, Abel. Talk to me."

"Suspicions about me. Us."

"What do you mean, *us*?" Cullen pointed his finger at Abel and then at himself. "Like in *us*? You and me?"

"I'm sorry. I was really paranoid after the night I'd had, and I know it makes no sense, but I just lost it. Okay?"

"Okay. Okay." Cullen forced a smile. "I guess I can see how you made the connection. Not sure I agree with it, but I can at least understand it."

"Thank you."

"Don't thank me yet. I have more questions."

"How did I already know that?" Abel's lips curled into a half smile.

Cullen chuckled. He didn't really know Abel, and Abel certainly didn't know Cullen was gay, but Cullen needed to know what Abel thought of homosexuality. This could make or break whatever type of friendship they were developing, and well... he just needed to know. *Choose your words carefully. You're about to step onto thin ice.* "So. Were you more angry that you had to argue on behalf of homosexuality or that the entire congregation was against it?"

Abel looked like he was contemplating the question. Finally, he said, "I don't really know the answer to that. I mean... I've been taught all my life that homosexuality is a sin and all homosexuals will burn in hell."

"But in some denominations, so will people who dance or drink alcohol."

"True," Abel said. "Mine, to be exact."

"What do *you* believe, Abel?"

Abel looked like he was about to answer when an elderly lady walked in front of their bench holding a small plastic bag in one hand and her cocker spaniel's leash in the other. "Pastor Weston?"

Abel jumped to his feet. "Mrs. Whitley. Good morning. So nice to see you out and about this fine Saturday. Hello, Chester." Abel petted the dog on the head.

"Likewise."

Mrs. Whitley looked at Cullen and cleared her throat as the dog squatted to the left of the sidewalk and started doing his business.

"Oh, forgive me," Abel said, apparently unaware of the dog's grunts. "This is my... my...."

Cullen waited.

"...friend Cull—"

"Reverend Kiley," Cullen said, cutting Abel off and getting to his feet.

Mrs. Whitley smiled, batted her sparse gray eyelashes, and tucked away the stray silver hairs escaping her bun. "Oh, how nice, a reverend. And I do apologize for Chester. He's very finicky about where he poops, and this just happens to be his favorite spot."

Mrs. Whitley opened the plastic bag and attempted to stoop down and pick up Chester's droppings.

Abel took the plastic bag. "Oh, here. Let me do that."

She smiled gratefully at Abel and turned to Cullen. "Southern Baptist, I hope?" she asked.

"No. Episcopal, actually," Cullen said.

The woman's smiled faded, and her face appeared to harden just a little. "Welcome to Southport, Reverend Kiley. I hope to see you at Sunday service tomorrow morning. Good day, gentlemen."

Mrs. Whitley straightened her shoulders, left Abel holding the bag of poop, and huffed off, dragging Chester down the sidewalk.

"Good day, Mrs. Whit...." Abel's voice trailed off when he was sure she could no longer hear him.

"Is this what you deal with on a regular basis?"

Abel nodded and looked around for a trash can. "Day in and day out. In all fairness, not every member of the congregation is like that. But most of the seniors were all raised with fire and brimstone. And to them there is only one Word. One truth."

"I don't know why anyone would associate with a church that is so judgmental and not welcoming to everyone and all walks of life."

Abel walked to the trash can, then glanced over his shoulder. "It's all I know. I'm a very spiritual person, and the Southern Baptists accepted me as a teenager. When I decided to serve God, doing it in the Southern Baptist Church came naturally. I mean... it was all I knew."

Cullen decided to let that one go. For now.

Abel tossed the poop bag and came back. He sat down and crossed his leg at the knee. Cullen sat as well. "So where were we?" Abel asked.

Cullen knew exactly where they were. "We were interrupted before you got a chance to answer my question."

"What question?"

"I asked what *your* thoughts are regarding homosexuality."

"I already told you how I was raised and what my church believes."

"If you ask me, I think you're avoiding the question."

More silence.

This was suddenly very important to Cullen. He wasn't going to let it go. "Come on, Abel. What *do* you believe?"

Abel was starting to fidget. His hands were resting in his lap, and he was rubbing them together, over and over. He finally said, "I don't know what to believe. I mean… I don't want to believe that homosexuals will burn in hell, and I don't want to believe God hates them, but I just don't know. I struggle with this every day, Cullen."

I struggle with this every day. The words rang through Cullen's head over and over. *Why does he struggle with this? Because of his beliefs and his church? Or could Abel be questioning his own sexuality?*

Cullen's thoughts were interrupted when Abel spoke again. "I did some research last night on the Episcopal Church and their beliefs."

Cullen sat up straight. *Can't wait to hear this.* "And what did you find out?"

"Well, for starters, back in 1976, the General Convention of the Episcopal Church declared that 'homosexual persons are children of God who have a full and equal claim with all other persons upon the love, acceptance, and pastoral concern and care of the Church.' Since then, faithful Episcopalians have been working toward a greater understanding and radical inclusion of all of God's children. And I know there are gay priests and even gay bishops."

I'm impressed. Cullen nodded. "You did do your homework."

"So your church welcomes everyone with open arms."

"Yes and no," Cullen said. "It's not that simple. And for the record, it's no longer *my* church. But to clarify, the Episcopal Church welcomes all to worship who have good intentions and pure hearts. We are all sinners, so the church also welcomes people with not so pure hearts, but who are repenting for sins committed. Rehabilitating, so to speak. But everyone—and I mean everyone, no matter who they love—is held to the same clean-living standards. In other words, homosexuals are held to the same standards as heterosexuals. Repenting thieves and doctors alike, all to the same standards. The main mission of the church is to restore all people to unity with God. Does that make sense?"

Abel's face lit up. "Of course it makes sense. It makes perfect sense." Abel glanced at his watch. "Damn! Where did the time go? I'm so sorry, Cullen. I've got ten minutes to get to the church to meet with a bride and groom about their upcoming wedding."

Abel laid his hand on Cullen's thigh and then nervously looked down at his hand like he wished he hadn't done that. But to his credit, he didn't yank it away. He raised his head until their eyes met. "I know we just met, and I have no idea why, but I haven't opened up to anyone like this before. You're just... nonjudgmental and so easy to talk to. Please, don't go. I really wish you would stay on a little longer."

Cullen broke their gaze and looked out over the water. He realized Abel had opened up a great deal today, but he was convinced there was more. Maybe, just maybe, if he continued to work with Abel, Cullen might get the entire story. His gut told him Abel was struggling with his sexuality and trying to fit into a church and a religion that had no tolerance for anyone who didn't fit their predetermined image of a good Christian. And in Cullen's opinion, if Abel was struggling with his sexuality, he was in a no-win situation. *I can't leave him high and dry.*

When Cullen looked at Abel once more, Abel was watching him with hopeful eyes. The sweetest, most beautiful, hopeful emerald-green eyes he'd ever seen. Cullen didn't have the heart to disappoint him. "Okay."

"You'll stay?"

"Sure. I'll stay a little longer. Under one condition."

Abel smiled. "Name it?"

"We continue to talk openly," Cullen said. "If we're going to be friends, you need to promise to be completely honest with me."

Abel's smile suddenly faded, and he started gnawing on his bottom lip. He appeared to be seriously contemplating Cullen's condition and what the end result might be. Hesitantly, Abel smiled again and finally whispered, "I promise. But... it's a two-way street. If I'm gonna be completely honest with you, then I expect the same in return. No more 'it's a long story' as an answer."

"Fair enough." Cullen smiled. "Okay, I know you need to go, but why don't you come to my boat tonight? I'll prepare dinner, and we can talk more."

"Okay," Abel said.

"Dock C. Three-quarters of the way down on the right. The boat's name is *T-Time*."

"You a golfer or royalty?"

"Neither. In the T-shirt business."

Abel stood. "Oh. Got it. What time?"

"Six thirtyish?"

"See you then. Bye, Cullen."

Abel walked away with a little pep in his step.

"Abel!" Cullen yelled. "Anything you don't eat?"

Abel looked back over his shoulder. "Nope."

CHAPTER FIVE

CULLEN REMAINED on the park bench long after Abel had left, mesmerized by the way the sun shimmered off of the waves, making the Southport Inlet appear to be an ocean of sparkling Swarovski crystals. It was mildly blinding but beautiful at the same time.

Cullen was stretched out, hands linked behind his head, trying to enjoy the warmth of the fall sunshine, but the word *stupid* kept interrupting his relaxation. Then it hit him. *What did I just agree to? I'm the one who's supposed to be helping Abel with his life, and now I just agreed to be completely honest with him about mine. You know what that means. Telling him you're gay, about why you left the church, and the hardest part, opening up about Cole.*

"Stupid!" he cursed under his breath.

But in all fairness, how could he expect Abel to be honest with him if he wasn't honest with Abel? Didn't a friendship work both ways? Did they have a friendship? Maybe the beginnings of one. But if Cullen hadn't opened up to anyone about Cole in the last year and a half—or why he'd left the church for that matter—why did he think he was ready to do it now?

After about an hour of figuratively smacking himself on the forehead over and over again for getting himself in this situation, Cullen gave up and left the familiarity of his park bench and the Riverwalk behind. He strolled toward the marina but stopped when he reached North Howe and heard the sound of children's laughter.

Something about the sound instantly transported Cullen back to the Church of Saint Mary of the Harbor in P-town and the children's Sunday morning Bible study. He felt his lips begin to curl at the edges until a full-on smile consumed his face. He remembered the sounds he'd heard every Sunday morning before service as parents dropped off their two- to five-year-olds. "Bible study" for them was more like arts and crafts time, but the themes always surrounded stories from the Bible, and the kids really loved it. Most Sundays, right after service, Cullen would say good-bye to his congregation, and he and Cole would run down to the basement classroom and spend a little time with the youngsters.

Without fail, when they reached the halfway point in the stairwell, he and Cole would hear the children's laughter coming from the classroom. The laughter today, much like back then, warmed his heart. He and Cole had always wanted children.

No! Determined not to ruin this moment, Cullen mumbled. "I'll leave that disappointment for another time."

Cullen looked at his watch and decided he had time to take a little detour. He followed the laughter and the aroma of grilling hot dogs and hamburgers until he reached a quaint little square. On the corner was a sign that read Franklin Square Park. In the center of the space stood a small gazebo, and he noticed a young couple setting up for what looked like a puppet show. There were at least two dozen little children running around and jumping up and down in anticipation.

Lingering at the edge of the park, Cullen stopped and took in the scene. It could have been Anytown, USA. The massive moss-covered oak trees spread over the grounds like a natural green leafy canopy. Underneath, picnic blankets spread out everywhere, and moms entertained toddlers and infants while dads played ball with the older children. It looked like a scene right off a Hallmark greeting card. Suddenly trumpets sounded, and all the kids stopped what they were doing and ran to the gazebo. They instantly settled down in front of the small puppet stage and waited patiently.

Apparently not *their first time at a puppet show!*

Music started to play, the curtain went up, and two marionettes dressed like a young prince and princess started singing and dancing, bowing and leaping. Cullen smiled as the kids squealed with delight. Everyone was having such a great time. A seemingly perfect Saturday morning in a perfect little town, with perfect little families, all leading their perfect little lives.

A stab of the familiar pain hit Cullen hard. His mood quickly turned solemn, and he was once again reminded of how much he'd lost. He had no husband, no children, not even his faith. Losing faith and leaving his church had been as hard as losing Cole. The church had been his life until God added Cole to it.

And then took him away, Cullen reminded himself. God and his church had turned their backs on him, and now he had nothing.

Am I crazy? What kind of person begrudges people who are living and enjoying their lives? His smile disappeared. *Crazy, bitter people! Just! Like! You!*

In danger of being suffocated by the loneliness and emptiness, he turned and started walking away. As the aromas, music, and laughter faded into the background, Cullen's first thought was to go back to the marina, ready his boat, and simply shove off. Charleston was looking better and better, and he could escape all of this if he just left. That was his plan for a few blocks. At least until his rational brain reminded him that he would be doing exactly what he'd done for the last year and a half: running away! And hadn't he told himself over and over he was tired of running? Wasn't that the reason for this trip, to try and bury his demons and attempt to get on with his life?

And what about Abel? Cullen had initiated this, whatever it was, and he'd promised he would stay in Southport a little while longer, so he couldn't turn his back on Abel. Not now. That would be no different from God turning his back on Cullen. Abel needed something to hold on to. And Cullen realized he did as well. Cullen's faith was already gone, but maybe he could help Abel hang on to his.

BY THE time Cullen reached his boat, his mood had improved, but only slightly. He was still alone and bitter, and his endless mood swings were getting the best of him.

Although he was really trying to get his life back on track, the oddest things set him off, and he was beginning to think he would never feel well or whole again. He had turned into a sullen Jekyll and Hyde, and he loathed himself for it.

Luckily, he'd once again talked himself off of the proverbial cliff. As he sat in the saloon feeling sorry for himself, he made an attempt to focus his attention on what he *had* instead of everything he didn't have. *You have a nice home in P-town. You have a thriving business. You have* T-Time. *And Cole left you set for life. You have so much more than most!*

It dawned on Cullen that maybe he did want to do better for himself. And if he were being honest, he thought that Abel might have something to do with that. Abel needed him. And above all right now, Cullen needed to be needed.

Abel! Suddenly remembering he'd invited Abel to dinner, Cullen rummaged through the galley. He was running low on supplies, so he made a grocery list, showered, and took the marina's courtesy car to the local Food Lion to buy supplies. Since he'd agreed to stay a few more days, he bought enough groceries to last until then, and he would deal with the next leg of his trip when the time came.

When Cullen returned, he put his groceries away, straightened the saloon, and cleaned the heads. When all his chores were done, he was exhausted. He glanced at the clock: 4:15.

Cullen lay across his bed, intending to only close his eyes for a few minutes, but his body had other plans.

Cullen was again sinking into the dark abyss. His lungs were already filled to capacity with cold, salty seawater, and after the initial shock and the flailing that ensued, his body settled down and accepted its fate. It was just a matter of time now before his brain followed the rest of his body and started to shut down.

He blinked twice against the dark, murky water, and a shred of hope momentarily filled his heart. Cole! He could vaguely see Cole, an arm's length away, sinking along with him. Cole had a soothing and peaceful smile on his face, and despite the iciness of the water, it warmed Cullen to his core.

Cullen used his last bit of energy and reached out for Cole. To be holding on to each other when they sank to their final resting place together was Cullen's last hope. But as he had been for the last year and a half, Cole was always just out of reach. But wait. Not this time. Cole reached out to him and took both of Cullen's hands in his. He mouthed, "Not your time, love. Live!" Cole looked up to the surface.

Cullen tried to make his lips form a word. One word: "No!" But it was no use. He was barely hanging on to life. Suddenly a smiling

Abel appeared next to Cullen and hovered, like an angel of sorts. Abel's expression was filled with such compassion and love that it confused Cullen. Cole placed both of Cullen's hands into Abel's and smiled. "Live!"

Abel propelled Cullen toward the surface. Cullen wanted to fight, but he had no energy. He didn't want to leave Cole. Didn't want to live without him. He kept looking down as he was being forced to the surface. Cole was disappearing, getting smaller and smaller but still looking up, arms stretched, smiling. "Live," kept reverberating in Cullen's brain. He and Abel broke the surface.

Cullen sat bolt upright in bed, gasping for air. He grabbed his throat and sucked in several ragged breaths. Forcing himself to relax, he inhaled deeply and slowly until his breathing was again under control. His eyes were wet with tears, and his hands were shaking. He jumped out of bed and paced nervously.

"What the hell was that about?"

His brain was on overload. Cullen had no capacity to even attempt to analyze that dream, so he went to the head and splashed cold water on his face. He passed the hand towel over his features and stared at his reflection in the mirror. His eyes were swollen and red, and his skin looked pale and almost pasty white.

Jeez, Cullen! What's happened to you?

With no answers other than the obvious, Cullen decided to call Abel and cancel their dinner. He was in a foul mood and wouldn't be good company for anyone, let alone a man of the cloth. But then he remembered he and Abel had never exchanged telephone numbers. *Use your head, Cullen! What about a telephone book? Directory assistance?* He picked up his phone and dialed 411. Then he cursed under his breath and ended the call when he couldn't remember Abel's last name. *Wyatt? Wesley? Webber? Oh hell, just forget about it.*

Almost on autopilot Cullen ventured to the galley, seasoned two filet mignon steaks with salt, pepper, and a little Worcestershire, and set them on the counter to come to room temperature. He poked holes in two potatoes, wrapped them in foil, and seasoned and doused some asparagus in olive oil. Prep done, Cullen went back to his cabin and made his bed. With nothing more to do, he sat on the edge. He ran his hands over his face and rubbed his eyes.

Cullen, you're barely making it through each day, but with each one you do get through, you're spiraling a little more out of control. This has got to stop or you're not going to survive.

CHAPTER SIX

"THIS IS as good as it gets." Abel looked at himself in the mirror one last time. He was wearing khaki shorts, boat shoes, and a turquoise polo shirt that, as someone in his congregation had commented, made his eyes look more blue than green. He leaned into the mirror and stared at his eyes, but he couldn't see it. *Oh, well!* Vanity had never been one of his sins, but tonight for some reason, he wanted to look especially nice. He stepped back from the full-length mirror and closed his closet door.

With a bounce in his step, Abel ran down the stairs of his two-story, church-owned bungalow on Caswell Avenue, his footsteps echoing on the hardwood floors of the big empty house. Abel grabbed a bottle of wine off the kitchen counter and opened his front door.

When he'd stopped at the wine store and asked about a nice wine, the skeptical eye of the cashier, who just happened to attend his church, was daunting. While the woman had helped him make his selection, Abel had explained that he was a guest at someone's house for dinner and wanted to bring a gift. Her scowl had softened a little, but she'd still eyed him warily. Was there nothing he could do in this town without falling under the watchful eyes of his congregation? He shrugged it off. *Comes with the territory, I guess.* Abel slid the key into the lock and turned the deadbolt.

The distance to the marina was just a few blocks, and it was a beautiful evening, so Abel decided to walk. Besides, it would give him a little time to decide how he was going to be completely honest with Cullen and still keep a certain little something to himself. He wanted to be honest—he really did. Only some things were just too personal to talk about. But he'd promised Cullen, and he would figure out a way to keep that promise and stay true to himself at the same time.

Abel looked at his watch when he reached the marina. *Six thirty-eight. I guess that constitutes six thirtyish.* His heart rate increased a little as he took a step onto the ramp leading to Dock C. As he hesitantly strolled down the dock, Abel noted all the boat names and stopped when he saw *T-Time*.

I wonder what the protocol is when you visit someone's boat. Do you yell "Ahoy"? Knock? Or just step onboard? He felt silly yelling "Ahoy," and he didn't think he knew Cullen well enough to just step onboard, so he knocked a couple of times on the hull.

Cullen's muffled voice came from somewhere deep inside the boat. Abel struggled but couldn't make out what Cullen had said, so he said the first thing that came to his mind. "Permission to come aboard, Captain?" Then he smacked himself in the forehead. *What a Dork!*

Cullen's voice was louder now and clearer. "Permission granted. Now get your butt up here!"

Abel stepped onto the boat and climbed up five steps to a carpeted area of about ten-by-fourteen feet. The area had wraparound seating, a bar and sink, and what appeared to be an icemaker. Three more steps up led to a higher level with even more seating, but it also appeared to be the helm. The dash was covered in black canvas, but he could clearly see the outline of a steering wheel under the cover.

An already half-open, tinted-glass doorway slid the rest of the way open. "Hey." Cullen popped his head out. "Welcome aboard."

The first thing Abel noticed was that Cullen didn't appear to be himself, at least the little he knew about the man. He was smiling, but the usual sparkle wasn't in his eyes.

"Come on in," Cullen said.

Abel followed Cullen down a set of stairs into a living room of sorts. He knew it was called something else on a boat, but he couldn't think of what it was. It was beautiful, though. High-gloss woodwork, hardwood floors with a large Oriental rug, and creamy beige leather couches lining the walls.

Abel shook Cullen's hand. "This is really nice." He continued to look around.

"Thanks. Help yourself if you'd like a tour. This is the saloon."
Saloon. Yeah, that's it.

Cullen waved and then gestured over his shoulder. "The galley. Two cabins and a head forward, and the master cabin and master head aft."

"Now, a head is a bathroom. Right?"

"Yes, sir."

Abel did the self-guided tour while Cullen fiddled in the galley. There were indeed two cabins. One with two beds and one with what looked like a queen-size bed forward. Also a bathroom, or head as Cullen had called it. *I had no idea there was so much space on a boat!*

He then moved across the saloon and walked down three steps into another cabin. This one was quite large, with a king-size bed. *This must be Cullen's cabin.* Abel ran his hand along the bed, and an image of Cullen lying there flashed through his mind. He blushed, feeling almost like a voyeur, and quickly shook the image from his mind's eye. There was also a dressing area and two doors. He opened each and found one was a shower and the other a water closet. Abel closed the door and realized he was still carrying the bag with the wine in it. He figuratively smacked himself in the forehead again.

"I'm no wine expert, but the lady at the wine store recommended this." Abel handed Cullen the blue bag.

"Thanks." Cullen took the bag, placed it on the counter, and went back to putting some cheese on a plate.

Abel knew for sure now that Cullen didn't seem to be in the mood for company. "I feel like I'm intruding. If tonight isn't convenient, we can certainly do it another time. No hard feelings."

Cullen looked up, and their eyes met. For the first time, Abel realized how handsome Cullen was. His host was wearing a black V-neck T-shirt, blue jeans riding low on his hips, and he was barefoot. The black shirt looked great with his dark hair and emphasized the hint of silver at his temples. And his brilliant eyes, albeit not as bright as they were in the morning sunshine, were a very deep blue just the same. Abel's thoughts were interrupted by the sound of Cullen's voice.

"No. I'm sorry. It's just... well, it's been a difficult day. Don't go."

"I'm sorry... but Cullen, really? If you want to be alone, I get it."

Cullen stepped up from the galley and laid a hand on Abel's shoulder. "That's one of the problems. I've been alone too much, and I'm getting sick of it. Please stay."

Abel didn't want to go, but he didn't want to intrude either. "Okay, but only if you insist."

"I insist. And thank you. Now, how would you like a glass of that wine?"

Abel hesitated. "No, thank you. But I will take a glass of water."

Cullen sighed. "Damn. I'm so stupid. I forgot. You don't drink."

"Never tried the stuff," Abel admitted.

Cullen opened the fridge. "I have club soda, cranberry juice, and orange juice."

"I think I'll have a combination of all three. That is if it's not too much trouble."

"Not at all."

While Cullen mixed Abel's drink, Abel looked around the boat some more. He studied a photograph hanging on the wall of a family of four. He knew right away it had to be a picture of Cullen's family. He looked just like his father and definitely had his mother's smile. "This has to be your family."

"Yep. That's my mom and dad, my little sister, Elaina, and me on Easter Sunday. I was eight."

"Are you a close family?"

"We used to be. My father died almost two years to the day after that photo was taken."

"Can I ask of what?"

Cullen handed Abel his drink. "Lung cancer. He was a chain smoker. In fact, he had cancer at the time that photo was taken. He just didn't know it then."

"I'm really sorry. And your mom?"

"She was killed about six years ago in a car accident."

"Oh, Cullen. Now I see why you're on the outs with the Almighty."

Cullen laughed sarcastically. "You haven't heard the half of it."

"I'd like to," Abel said sincerely, taking a sip of this drink. "This is good. Thank you. What are you having?"

"A little bourbon on the rocks. Episcopalians are allowed to drink, especially former Episcopalians."

Abel laughed. "It's a good thing I don't. I believe if I started in my current state, I might not stop. And that wouldn't be good for my career."

Cullen placed a plate of cheese and fruit on the table. "Help yourself."

Abel did help himself and continued looking around with a cracker in hand. He studied all the pictures closely, and every other picture was of Cullen and an extremely good-looking man with sandy-blond hair. They were touching in one way or another in every photograph and smiling broadly. It appeared they were very happy and quite comfortable together.

When Abel looked in Cullen's direction, Cullen was leaning against the refrigerator, feet crossed at the ankle, sipping on his drink and watching him closely. He had a dark and brooding expression on his face, and Abel was concerned. "Everything okay?" Abel asked.

"It depends."

Taken aback by that comment, Abel asked, "On what?"

"Whether you're gonna ask me about the person in all those photographs."

"I won't if you don't want me to."

"Not just yet, if you don't mind. I think I need another couple shots of bourbon before we go down that road."

Abel nodded. Little things were starting to add up, and Abel had a pretty good idea who Cullen was, but he would leave it alone for now and let Cullen tell him when he was ready. It seemed they both had secrets.

CHAPTER SEVEN

ABEL LEANED back and rubbed his stomach, feeling more full then he had in a very long time. "You're an excellent grill master," he said. "And I insist you allow me to clean." He stood, gathered their plates and silverware, and carried them across the saloon to the galley.

Cullen also leaned back, rested his arm across the back of the banquette, and took a sip of the red wine Abel had contributed to the dinner. "You'll get no arguments from me on that front. I hate doing dishes." He held up the glass. "And this is really good, by the way."

Abel had explained the reaction he'd received from the clerk at the wine store over dinner. "For someone who supposedly doesn't drink, she sure knew her red wine."

Dinner conversation had mostly consisted of a lot of small talk. Some discussion about the Southern Baptist Church and their beliefs compared to the Episcopal Church. Huge differences, to say the least, but they both seemed to be avoiding anything too heavy. But something seemed different to Abel. The ease they'd shared at the Riverwalk was no longer there, and honestly, Abel missed the connection.

Cullen was on his third glass of wine—not that Abel was counting—but Abel could tell Cullen's mood seemed to be improving. It was either Abel or the alcohol or maybe a combination of both, but Cullen did seem more at ease.

While Abel did the dishes, he could see Cullen eyeing him, almost like he had something to get off of his chest but was unsure if he could do it. Maybe it was about the guy in the picture or quite possibly about his day, which he'd already said had sucked.

Abel dried and stacked the last plate, dried his hands, and folded the towel and laid it on the edge of the sink. "Do you mind if I get a bottle of water out of the fridge?"

"Help yourself." Cullen stood, crossed the saloon, and slipped behind Abel into the small galley.

Abel bent over, dug through the refrigerator, and froze when he felt Cullen brush against his backside and Cullen's hand rest briefly on his hip. The feeling was both exhilarating and frightening at the same time. Abel closed his eyes and focused on trying not to jump or pull away.

"Sorry," Cullen said. "It's a tight space. I mark a great boater by whether or not a person can do what we call the galley dance."

"Galley dance?" Abel repeated, now a bit intrigued.

Cullen retrieved a rocks glass and poured himself a couple of fingers of bourbon. "Yeah. The galley dance is when two people can get into a rhythm and easily move and work together in the small space in unison. Cole and I had it down to a science."

Cole! Is that the name of the man in the photos? The elephant in the room?

It suddenly dawned on Abel that the Riverwalk had been neutral ground for them. It had been easy to connect there. They could give a little at a time and keep what they weren't ready to share without being too exposed. But here—this boat—was Cullen's home. His memories. His life. No wonder he was distant. There was no hiding here for him. Cullen was very exposed and vulnerable.

Abel thought about what it would feel like to have Cullen at his home. To actually see his sad existence. His lack of family photos. Hell, his lack of photos of any kind. The nonexistence of anything that was actually his. Everything in the house but his clothes and his computer equipment was owned by the church, and he lived under their rules.

With that realization Abel decided to let the comment go, and if Cullen wanted to bring the man up again, he would.

"Abel?"

Abel was startled out of his thoughts by the sound of Cullen's voice.

"Are you okay?"

"Oh, yeah. Sorry. No. I'm good."

He could see Cullen eyeing him warily.

"No really. I'm good."

"Okay. Let's go topside and enjoy the rest of the evening."

"Lead the way, Captain," Abel teased.

Abel followed Cullen up the steps to what he learned was called the cockpit and then up to the flybridge or helm. Cullen took a seat, and Abel looked around. "Do you mind?" Abel gestured to the canvas.

"Not at all."

Abel unsnapped the canvas and lifted it off the helm equipment. It was all very intimidating. "This looks like the cockpit of a 747."

Cullen chuckled. The sound was warm and seemed to come from a place deep down. This was the Cullen he knew. "It looks way more intimidating than it is."

"Really?"

"Really." Cullen pointed to the different pieces of equipment. "This is the GPS unit. This is the depth finder, and this is the autopilot."

"What are these?" Abel pointed to the various gauges.

"Voltage meter. Temperature gauge. Oil pressure gauge. And as you can see, there's one for each engine."

Abel nodded. "What are these things?"

"Oh, various stuff. Horn. Bilge pumps. Lights. Windlass anchor controls. Search light controls. Stabilizer controls."

"Stabilizer controls?"

"Yeah. You can lower or raise the bow depending on the height and direction of the seas. Or you can balance your load from port to starboard so she rides evenly in the water."

"I'm very impressed." And Abel meant it. There were a lot of buttons and gauges to master, and it was obvious Cullen was an experienced captain.

Abel replaced the canvas and snapped it back into place. He took a seat in the curve of the couch and sipped his water. The marina was quiet except for the distant sounds of what Cullen explained were lanyards or rigging tapping against the masts of the many sailboats in the harbor, moving gently in the light breeze. The constant flash of the Oak Island Lighthouse reminded Abel that he was never far from home. The sounds of the marina and the rhythmic movement of the boat were very soothing, and he could see why Cullen liked being on the water. Abel finally started to relax.

"Cole was my husband," Cullen said unexpectedly.

"What?" Abel said, caught off guard.

"The guy in the picture. Cole. He was my husband."

Cullen stared at Abel hesitantly, as if he half expected him to run or to try to exorcise him or something.

"*Was* your husband?" Abel managed to say in an even tone and with as little surprise in his voice as possible. In fact he wasn't surprised. In their pictures they were too comfortable together to be anything but lovers.

"He died."

Abel decided to allow Cullen to take the lead. This was obviously very difficult for Cullen, and he wanted to make it as easy as possible. After all, Cullen was in essence coming out to a Southern Baptist minister. That in itself took balls.

"I'm very sorry for your loss."

A few minutes of silence trickled by, and then Cullen finally asked, "Is that all you're gonna say? Aren't you gonna tell me I'll burn in hell and jump overboard before I try and take advantage of you, or even worse, try to convince you to take a trip on the wild side?"

Abel did his best to stifle a laugh. "Not hardly."

A seemingly reluctant smile landed on Cullen's lips. "Thanks for that."

"Will you tell me about him?"

As Abel waited patiently, Cullen swirled the caramel colored liquid in his glass and stared at it like it might be the courage he so desperately needed. He finally took a sip and then looked out over the water and closed his eyes as if he were traveling back in time. When he finally spoke, his voice was low and gravelly. "I had completed my discernment, graduated the seminary, been ordained, and had just completed two six-month runs as a transitioning diaconate when I was finally assigned my first cure, or ministry. It was at the Church of St. Mary of the Harbor in Provincetown, MA. I was more than ready, and being openly gay, I was thrilled to be assigned to P-town, where gayness flowed like Niagara Falls."

Cullen paused, and Abel took advantage of the silence. "Is P-town some gay mecca or something?"

"You could say that," Cullen opened his eyes and chuckled. "At the time, it was mostly gays and sixties throwbacks, or hippies who were all destined to save something or other. Trees, whales, patchouli. You get the idea. I mean, don't get me wrong. They were lovely, generous, warm, and accepting people, and I loved my congregation dearly, but some of them were a little out there."

Abel nodded. "I'm sorry for the interruption. Please go on."

"On my first Sunday in my new parish, I saw him sitting in the fourth row, third person from the end. He was the most handsome man I had ever seen. I remember focusing on his hair for some odd reason. It was a beautiful, almost golden color. Not quite blond, not quite brown, shoulder-length with sunstruck blond highlights, and he wore it parted slightly off-center, combed back and behind his ears. His looks were striking, really. So much so that I had a hard time not staring at him throughout the entire mass."

Cullen closed his eyes again and sighed. "He was wearing a navy blue suit and a gold-and-navy tie, and even from the sanctuary, I could see his vivid blue eyes looking up at me. When the mass was over and made its way down the aisle, our eyes met and he smiled. And... that's all it took. I was hooked."

Cullen opened his eyes and took another sip of his bourbon. "It seems like a lifetime ago."

"How long ago was it?"

"Oh, about eleven years or so now."

"You were together a long time, then?" Abel asked.

"Almost nine years."

"Wow! So what happened next?"

Cullen smiled. "Well, I exited the church, greeted and chatted with my new congregation, and periodically glanced around hoping to catch a glimpse of him. Eventually the crowds started thinning, and I'd almost given up hope. I said good-bye to the last couple, and when they passed me by, I spotted him standing off to the side, waiting for me. I swear my heart almost leapt right out of my chest."

"Was he your first?" Abel asked.

"Sexual partner? No. First and only love? Absolutely."

"And?"

"We chatted on the steps of the church until we both got tired of standing, and then I finally took the bull by the horns and invited him back inside. We sat in one of the pews and talked for almost two more hours."

Cullen's eyes were closed again, and he was smiling fondly. "He was born and raised right there on the Cape and, after graduating UMass, had moved to P-town, where he bought a small T-shirt shop on Commercial Street. A couple years later, his shop was doing so well, he bought a house three blocks from the church, and he'd made a nice little life for himself. He'd not found that special someone, which was music to my ears, but he was certainly open to it. He loved children, was a runner and an avid boater. In fact, he's the reason we're sitting on this boat right now. Anyway, we dated exclusively for almost a year, and as soon as marriage was legal in Massachusetts, we tied the knot. Man! We had it all. Until...."

Cullen stopped short of finishing his sentence. He opened his eyes and chugged the rest of his drink. "If I'm gonna get through this story, I'm gonna need more bourbon."

"Can I have some too?" Abel shocked himself.

"Sure, but don't hold me responsible for corrupting the pastor."

"No one's corrupting the pastor," Abel snorted. "I'm thirty-five years old. I think I have a right to taste bourbon if I want to."

Cullen apparently conceded because he came back up with two glasses. "Take it slow," Cullen warned. "It may burn a little."

Abel brought the glass to his lips and dipped his tongue into the rich brown liquid. "Sweet. Strong. So good." Then Abel took a sip. As the liquid slid down his throat, he felt the burn Cullen had warned him about. It wasn't bad. In fact, it warmed him all the way down to his toes. "I like it. Probably a little too much."

Cullen frowned. "There goes the neighborhood."

"You shut up!" Abel said teasingly, surprising even himself. Then he took on a more serious expression. "If Cole is too difficult to talk about, I understand. I mean... I get it, man. We all have things that are just too difficult to deal with or talk about."

"No. It's time. I need this. Besides, if I don't talk about it, I may just throw myself another pity party and drown in my own sorrows."

Abel's pastoral training took hold. "I'm here for you, then, and I'll do whatever I can to help you get through this."

"Thank you." Cullen shook his head. "Now where was I?"

"You guys were happy and everything was going great," Abel reminded him.

"Yeah. We saved up enough money to buy this boat, took our first trip south for the winter—all the way to Key West, Florida. On our way back up, we stayed at this very marina for a few days."

Cullen explained how the movie crew was filming *Safe Haven* and told Abel about how much fun they'd had, which was why he was here now.

"So we got back to P-town at the end of March," Cullen explained. "Cole got the shop opened up and running, and we settled back into life. While we were away, Cole had organized a group of our church members to run the Provincetown 10K Charity race on June first, so we got our group together and started training immediately. In the last stretch of the race, Cole collapsed. Right in the middle of Route 6."

Cullen's voice started to crack. "We later found out he'd had a massive brain aneurism. He died in my arms, both of us still in the middle of the street."

Abel was silent as he watched Cullen wipe away the tears that were streaming down his face. He downed what was left of the bourbon and flinched, and Abel imagined the burn making its way down Cullen's throat. Whether it was the effects of the bourbon, the horrible story, or simply his compassion, he didn't know, but he slid over, sat next to Cullen, took the man into his arms, and cradled him as he cried.

Neither of them moved for the longest time, and Abel felt remarkably comfortable with Cullen in his arms. He allowed the man the time he needed to grieve, something Cullen had probably never done properly.

Abel rubbed Cullen's back and ran his fingers through Cullen's thick black hair, anything he could do to help comfort his grieving friend. How earth-shattering all this must have been for him. To lose his father, his mother, and then Cole. There was no question in Abel's mind about why Cullen felt God had turned his back on him.

Abel didn't think he would have felt any differently. But all his training, as well as Cullen's, taught them just the opposite. Taught them that God had a plan. He always had a plan, and human beings weren't privy to it. God had needed Cullen's parents and Cole, and it wasn't for them to understand. It was all part of the big picture.

But in this case, Abel just couldn't see it. What words could he find to help Cullen through this? Cullen wouldn't accept the usual "It's God's plan" speech, and Abel wouldn't give it. After all, he had his own issues with the big man. But he needed to say something. Make some sort of impact on his friend.

Cullen lifted his head off of Abel's shoulder, and Abel immediately wanted it back there. He liked the human contact. He liked Cullen.

"Sorry," Cullen said pulling his black T-shirt up to wipe his face.

Abel couldn't help but notice Cullen's taut, flat stomach, but he instinctively looked away. "No need to apologize. I know that couldn't have been easy for you. Thank you for trusting me enough to share it with me."

"It needed to be done. I've been holding all this in for so long I was close to an epic explosion."

Abel took Cullen's hand in his and looked him in the eyes. "I don't believe everything we've been taught. I don't believe in the big picture. God's plan. What I do believe is sometimes horrible things happen to wonderful people. I don't understand how some people are forced to endure so much pain while others experience so little. But that's not for me to understand. It just happens, and all I can do is help clean up the fallout."

Cullen squeezed Abel's hand. "Thank you for not giving me that 'God called them home' bullshit."

Abel couldn't help but smile a little. "I wish I had the words to take away some of your pain, but I don't think those words exist yet. Time, acceptance, proper grieving, and people who care about you are the only things that will see you through this."

"I've alienated everyone who cares or… cared for me," Cullen shared. "I've been so bitter."

"I'm sure that's not true. In fact, you haven't alienated me. I care for you, and I'm right here."

"Oh, yeah?" Cullen chuckled. "Give me enough time and I'll push you away just like I did the rest of them."

"What about Elaina?" Abel asked.

"I haven't spoken to her in a year. When our parents died and then Cole, she turned to her faith at the same time I turned away from mine. She couldn't understand why I was so angry at God or why I left the church. She does believe in the big picture and God's plan. She was always a little naïve, that one."

"Maybe she needs to believe in something so she can cope. Something to hold on to, so to speak. For some, without that something, the pain is too great to bear. Everyone grieves in his or her own way."

"I was trained, just as you were, to handle these situations, but I no longer see it that way."

"Yeah, but sometimes you're just too close to a situation to be able to see it clearly."

"Maybe," Cullen said.

Abel smiled. "You should reach out to her."

"Maybe sometime in the future. But not now. I'm not ready yet."

"Okay. But just keep it tucked away in the back of your mind. I feel certain she'll be there with open arms when you're ready."

They sat hand in hand for a few more minutes, the sounds of the marina surrounding them like a comfortable blanket. "I know it's getting late and you have church in the morning."

"I'm okay," Abel said. "I'm here as long as you need me."

"I'm the one who's supposed to be helping you, remember?"

"Maybe we were meant to help each other."

"Maybe," Cullen said. "But just the same, it's time for you to get out of here." Cullen stood and sat right back down again. "Whoa. I think I've had a little too much bourbon, and it's all gone to my head."

Abel stood. He too felt a little light-headed, so he could imagine what Cullen must feel like. "Here, let me help you."

He offered his hands to Cullen and pulled the man to his feet. Abel put one of Cullen's arms over his shoulder and held on to his hand. He slipped his other arm around Cullen's waist, and together they walked. They took the three steps to the cockpit very carefully and then worked their way through the companionway door. That one wasn't so easy for two grown men, but they eventually made it. By the time they reached Cullen's cabin, he was little to no help at all.

Abel all but carried him to the bed and sat him down. He pulled back the covers and fluffed the pillow. He gripped Cullen's T-shirt and pulled it over his head, biting his lip at the sight of his broad, well-defined chest with a sprinkle of hair between his pectoral muscles and a line of hair that ran down to his stomach and disappeared into his jeans. Abel swung Cullen's legs around and laid the man down gently. He thought about removing Cullen's jeans but didn't think he had the courage.

After pulling the covers up over Cullen and tucking him in, Abel went to Cullen's dressing area and opened the cabinet behind the mirror. He located a bottle of Advil. *He'll need these for sure tomorrow morning.* He then went to the galley, got a bottle of water, and placed the bottle of pills and the water on Cullen's bedside table. Cullen was out like a light.

Abel took the opportunity to study the man's face. Even in his sleep, he looked broken and troubled. His brows were furrowed, and his forehead was creased like he was in deep thought. This evening when Cullen opened up to him, Abel had understood his loss, and he could certainly relate to Cullen's feelings of abandonment.

With no other reason to stay, Abel turned to go. But he stopped suddenly, leaned down, closed his eyes, and pressed his lips against Cullen's forehead. He held them there for a few seconds. Cullen's skin was warm and soft, and it felt so good to have the human contact. "Good night, my new friend," he whispered. "Sleep well."

But Abel didn't straighten. His eyes trailed down Cullen's handsome face and stopped at Cullen's full lips. Without conscious thought Abel gingerly pressed his lips against Cullen's in a brief, gentle kiss. Cullen's lips were as satiny and sweet as he'd imagined they would—the one fleeting moment he'd allowed himself to imagine such a thing. "We have more in common than you'd ever imagine."

He stood, turned out the light, and closed the door behind him. In the saloon, he turned out all but one lamp, and then he closed the companionway door and walked down the steps to the dock. He looked back one last time and cursed himself.

After tonight, Abel, nothing can ever be the same again.

Chapter Eight

"What have I done?" Cullen rolled over and cursed under his breath. His first thought was to get up, look for the two-by-four someone had hit him over the head with last night, and then finish the job. But the getting up part would be too difficult and way too painful.

He opened his eyes and squinted against a cabin full of bright sunshine. *Morning or afternoon?* One glance at the clock told him it was after eleven. He brought his arm up to cover his eyes and wished like hell he was dead. His mouth was dry and as gritty as the Mojave. His head was pounding, and his stomach was churning and weak. *Need water.*

Rolling over as gently as possible, Cullen froze when he saw the Advil and a bottle of water on his bedside table. *Yes, Virginia, there is a drug fairy!* He pushed up and rested on his elbow, opened the bottle and poured three pills into his hand, popped them into his mouth, and downed the entire bottle of water. Cullen rolled over, buried his head in the pillow, and cursed the likes of bourbon forever.

The next time Cullen woke, he rolled over onto his back, raised his head gingerly, and took stock of his physical condition. He felt almost alive. Nowhere near good, but at least alive. The headache had subsided to a manageable level, and the water must have helped hydrate him, because his stomach felt more settled as well. He was actually hungry, which he thought was a good sign.

The light still came in from his cabin portholes, but the cabin itself wasn't nearly as bright as it had been the first time he'd woken. He rolled over and squinted to make out the numbers on the clock: 2:35.

Cullen sighed and sat up, swinging his feet to the floor. He was bare chested but still in his blue jeans. He rubbed his hands over his day-old beard. *You haven't tied one on like that in fifteen years.*

Sitting on the edge of the bed, he rested his head in his hands and struggled to put the pieces of last night's puzzle together.

The first thing he remembered was way too much bourbon. And the next was Abel. *Abel!*

The drug fairy. Oh, God help me. Abel must think I'm a complete lunatic.

I remember grilling the steaks, having dinner. Nothing out of the ordinary. Abel did the dinner dishes. We headed topside.

Little bits and pieces started to come back to him. *I came out to Abel.* More bourbon. *I told him about Cole.* A lot more bourbon. *Oh, and Abel had a glass of bourbon too. Shit! I corrupted a pastor.* And then Cullen's chest tightened as he remembered what happened next. Being held tightly in Abel's arms while he cried like a baby. *Way to go, Cullen! That's twice you've broken down since you arrived in this godforsaken town. And yes.* Cullen looked up. *I do mean God forsaken town.*

But wait. Cullen remembered more. How comforted he'd felt in Abel's arms. How understood and cared for, which was something he hadn't felt in such a long time. Abel had been so reassuring. And not the least bit judgmental.

Cullen lay down again, linked his fingers across his stomach, and looked up at the ceiling. *There's something else. But what?* Something important was just at the edge of his memory. It was peeking out but not fully revealing itself. *Think, Cullen. Think!* And then like the rush of a river, the memories started coming back to him. *Abel helped me to the cabin. He pulled my T-shirt over my head, and then he helped me into bed. But there's more. A kiss! No. Yes! It was a kiss. Abel kissed me on the forehead. But that's not all. Wait! Not only did he kiss me on the forehead, he also kissed me on the lips.*

Cullen brought his hand up and brushed his fingers lightly over his lips. His subconscious was trying to raise something else to the level of consciousness. Something major. "We have more in common than you'd ever imagine" rang through his head and kept repeating like Paul Revere announcing the British were coming.

The kiss. Those words. You were right. Abel all but came out to you last night. That's what he's struggling with.

Cullen sat up and got to his feet with renewed purpose. He needed to see Abel. He was going to help the man. Cullen's dream came back to him abruptly. *Maybe Cole handed me off to Abel because he knew Abel needed me.*

AFTER A shower and a bite to eat, Cullen decided on a run. He needed to wrap his head around everything that had happened in the last few days, and running always cleared his head.

Wow. Has it only been a few days? It feels so much longer.

But more importantly he needed to see Abel. He was worried Abel might be freaking out and wanted to make sure he was okay. And lastly he needed to get the bourbon out of his system, and sweating it out was probably the quickest way.

Cullen started out on his normal route, heading for the Riverwalk. His first hope was that Abel would be on his usual perch. If he was there after last night, he was either praying for forgiveness or begging God to make him straight. Either way Cullen would be there to try to make him see he didn't need forgiveness or to be straight, as if that were even possible. When Cullen rounded the corner and the swings and park benches came into view, there were people everywhere, enjoying the Sunday afternoon, but as he ran along the water's edge perusing every bench and swing, he caught no glimpse of Abel.

Where are you, Abel?

His next thought was to go straight to the church office, but it was Sunday, and the office would be closed. Besides, Abel would probably not be very comfortable with Cullen showing up at his church. So he did the only other thing he knew to do.

Abel had told him when they first met that he lived a few blocks from the marina, so Cullen started running down West Bay Street. When he hit North Howe, he turned left and then left again at the next block and ran all the way down to the water. He turned right and then right again all the way back up to North Howe, running a grid of the area around the Southport Marina.

Sure, he knew it was a longshot, but it *was* Sunday, and he imagined after the service, Abel would probably have the rest of the day off. And maybe—just maybe—Abel might be working in his yard or might be out for a walk, and they'd run into each other. He couldn't not do *something*, and short of this, there was little else he *could* do until tomorrow morning.

After almost seven miles of running up and down every street within a six block radius of the marina, Cullen was back at the Riverwalk. He slowed now to a stroll, scanning the park for Abel as he attempted to catch his breath, but there was still no sign of him. The last bit of hope he had of finding Abel today was that during his run he'd remembered Abel's last name. It was Weston. Abel Weston. As soon as he got back to the boat, he would look up Abel's landline, if he had one, or at least find his address. Southport was a small town. How hard could it be?

With no confirmed sighting of Abel at the Riverwalk, Cullen walked briskly back to the marina. Back aboard *T-Time*, Cullen grabbed a bottle of water and his computer and settled on the flybridge. He wasn't sure why he hadn't done this before, but he typed "Southport Baptist Church" into a Google search box. The first result showed a picture of the church, the address, and the telephone number. He clicked on it, and the church's website appeared on his screen with a big ad for Weeknight Worship and dinner every Wednesday night through the fall. Cullen then scanned the top of the page and moved his cursor over the Team button. A drop-down menu appeared with a Meet Our Team option. Cullen clicked on it and a list of names appeared. The senior pastor was first, and Abel's name was just below as Associate Pastor Abel Matthew Weston. *Matthew? Nice.*

To his dismay, all he was offered was an e-mail address. But at least he had Abel's middle name, and that might make his search a little easier. So he opened Google again and typed in "Pastor Abel Matthew Weston, Southport, North Carolina." The first thing to pop up was the church's website. Next came a link to a story in the local paper, the *State Port Pilot*, with the heading "Abel M. Weston joins Southport Baptist Church as Associate Pastor."

Cullen clicked on the link and saw Abel's smiling face looking back at him from where he sat on the front steps of the church. Cullen started reading the article.

A youthful new associate pastor named Abel
Matthew Weston has just joined the Southport Baptist

Church. Associate Pastor Weston graduated at the top of his class from the Southeastern Baptist Theological Seminary in Wake Forest, NC, with a Master of Divinity with Pastoral Ministry.

Associate Pastor Weston was born to an underage unwed mother and given up at birth, which resulted in him spending eighteen years in the North Carolina Foster Care system. According to Associate Pastor Weston, his treasured Bible is the only link he has to his birth mother. "This Bible belonged to my birth mother," said Weston. "As a young child, it's what I used to learn to read and is what has carried me through many dark times while I navigated from one home to another in the overburdened foster care system. It was the inspiration for my spiritual journey, and it and my faith mean the world to me," Weston added.

Associate Pastor Weston comes to Southport from the First Baptist Church of Raleigh, NC, where he studied under Senior Pastor John B. Hutch as a Minister of Missions.

"We are extremely thrilled to have Associate Pastor Weston join The Southport Baptist Church," said Senior Pastor Henry P. Williams. "His expertise and youth will be a perfect fit for our outreach programs, which are designed to develop and increase Southport's youths' participation in the church."

Associate Pastor Weston is currently single and will reside in the church-owned residence on Caswell Street in Southport.

Cullen closed the article with slightly renewed hope. *Caswell Street. I've seen that street. As a matter of fact, I've been on that street. Several times.* And then he sighed. *Wow, Abel, foster care? I had no idea. That must have sucked.*

After selecting a people search engine from Google, Cullen typed in Abel's full name and state, clicked search, and waited. Minutes later three Abel Matthew Westons came up, but they didn't show any information other than a name. When he clicked on the first option, the site asked for a credit card. *Free? Yeah, right.* Cullen entered his credit card information, and additional information regarding the first Abel appeared on the screen. This Abel graduated from Duke, was in the financial industry, lived in Charlotte, and was married with two children. *Definitely not him.* Cullen exited that record and clicked on the next Abel. This record showed a little more promise but not much. It did have this Abel as a graduate of the Southeastern Baptist Theological Seminary, which was correct, but the address listed was a Raleigh address. *This is an old record.* Cullen read on. Single. No children. *Damn!*

He exited that record and held his breath as he clicked on his last option. *Bingo!* Cullen became hopeful. *This has got to be him.* Associate Pastor Abel Matthew Weston, Southport Baptist Church, Southport, NC. *Wait, no!* The address listed was the church's address on North Howe Street. Cullen slammed his computer closed. *I guess since the church owns the residence, that must be his formal address.*

Certain something wasn't right and feeling more ill at ease by the minute, Cullen did the only thing he could do. He went back to Caswell Street. *It's Sunday afternoon. Someone's gotta be out in their yard or taking a walk. It's a small town—doesn't everyone know everyone in a small town?*

Cullen picked up his pace until he was almost jogging. He cut through Yacht Basin Street to Brunswick Street and turned left onto Caswell. He walked all the way up to North Howe and saw not one single soul in their yard, sitting on their porch, or simply taking a stroll. He crossed the street and started back down the other side of Caswell, keeping a sharp eye out.

Most of the houses in Southport, at least near the harbor, featured a plaque next to the front door with the formal name of the house and the year it was built. He'd read somewhere that the houses were usually named after the ship's captain who built them, but he also thought that maybe Abel's house, since it was owned by the church, might reference something religious as well. He knew it was another long shot, but as he walked along, he studied each plaque for any sign of the church. Cullen also paid attention to the details of the houses, looking for any small sign of Abel. He stopped at one house that had a pair of worn boat shoes at its front door. Cullen studied the shoes from the sidewalk to see if he recognized them as Abel's. But no such luck.

Cullen was nearing the last block of Caswell, and he was quickly losing hope. Until he spotted an elderly lady bending over and cutting dead roses off of a row of bushes against a white decorative fence. When she looked up, he smiled at her. "I'll bet those were beautiful during the summer months."

"They were indeed." The woman straightened and stretched her back. "But I think this may be my last year of doing this on my own. I'm just getting too old."

"I'm not much of a gardener, but I'd be happy to help if there's anything I can do."

The woman smiled appreciatively. "Oh, thank you. But I'm sure you have better things to do than help an old woman deadhead her roses."

Cullen realized he needed to keep the conversation going until he could work in his question about whether she knew Abel. But what? Then he took a page from Abel's book and used his retired profession to help him along. "I'm Reverend Cullen Kiley."

The woman brushed the strands of her gray hair behind her ear and pressed the front of her cotton dress. "Reverend Kiley. So nice to meet you. I'm Dorothy Arnold. But you can call me Dottie."

Cullen nodded shyly. His first thought was he didn't want to lie to this nice lady, but he knew he would have to stretch the truth a bit to get the answers he needed.

"Are you settling in Southport, Reverend?" she asked.

"No, ma'am. Just passing through on my boat." *Truth!* "I was told by a mutual friend that a buddy of mine who also went to the seminary lived near the marina in Southport. So I thought I'd stop here on my way down south and reconnect." *Sort of the truth! Not really. Okay, I lied a little. Fine! I lied a lot.*

"Oh could you be speaking of Abel—" She stopped and corrected herself. "I mean… Pastor Weston."

"As a matter of fact, I am," Cullen said. "Do you know him?"

"Of course I do. He's my neighbor."

"Now what are the odds of that?"

Dottie smiled. "Southport is a very small town, Reverend. I'm 106 Caswell Avenue, and he's 108." She gestured to the house next door.

Cullen followed her hand with his eyes and smiled when he saw a neatly maintained, two-story, medium-gray bungalow trimmed in white, complete with a matching white picket fence and front porch with rocking chairs. "Can't get a town much smaller than that," Cullen said absentmindedly.

He stepped back and took it all in. The house was bigger than he'd expected, but after careful consideration he thought it somehow fit Abel. It might belong to the church, but it had a *Mayberry R.F.D.* feel and matched Abel's boyish looks in an odd sort of way.

Cullen stuck out his hand. "Well, it was sure a pleasure to meet you, Ms. Arnold."

"Oh, Dottie, please," she said, smiling again. "Any friend of Abel's is a friend of mine. He's such a sweet boy. I swear to you, Reverend, I don't know why some pretty young girl hasn't scooped him up yet. I'll tell you—" She looked around to make sure no one was in earshot. "—if I was fifty years younger...." She blushed and batted her eyelashes. "Oh, shoot. There I go again with my wild imagination. My mother always said I had no filter between my brain and my lips. Just please forget I said that."

"Forget you said what?" Cullen winked.

Dottie smiled coyly and rested her hands on her tiny hips. "I like you, Reverend."

Holding her frail hand in his, Cullen leaned in and kissed her on the cheek. "I like you too. It was sure a pleasure. Now I'd better get over there and say hi to Abel before I run out of time. Enjoy the rest of your Sunday, Dottie."

"You too, Reverend."

Cullen followed the sidewalk to Abel's front gate. *I know why some pretty girl hasn't scooped him up yet.*

"Oh, Reverend," Dottie called out. "I was so caught up in our conversation, I almost forgot. Abel's not at home."

Cullen stopped and turned around, his feeling of anticipation disappearing quickly. "No?"

"I saw him leave this morning shortly after he returned from Sunday service."

Cullen's heart sank once again. "Did he happen to mention where he was going or when he'd be back?"

"Heavens, no," Dottie said. "I'm a good neighbor. Not a nosy one. I would never ask such questions."

"Of course not," Cullen said, hearing the disappointment in his own voice. "I didn't mean to insinuate. I was just hoping to see him before I left. That's all."

"I understand." Dottie's voice softened. "Would you like to wait here for him? I can make some tea, and I just baked a loaf of pumpkin bread this morning."

"That's very kind, but I've got to get back to my boat. Do you by any chance have his cell phone number?"

"I do, but…." Dottie said apprehensively. She was now biting the side of her mouth, and her expression was skeptical.

"Forgive me," Cullen said. "I shouldn't have even asked. That was rude of me."

"Oh, what the heck," Dottie finally said. "You're a friend of Abel's and a man of the cloth. What harm could it bring?"

"Thank you, Dottie."

CULLEN WAS back at the marina and sitting on *T-Time* fidgeting and checking his watch constantly. He'd called Abel while walking back to the marina. The phone rang four times and then went to voice mail. He left a message and waited. And waited. Two hours passed and still no return call. He'd tried again and the call went to voice mail again, so he hung up. Three more hours passed, and he called Abel's number again. "Damn, Abel! Where are you?" The phone went straight to voice mail once more.

By midnight Cullen gave up and went to bed. He tossed and turned for hours, contemplating Abel's situation and state of mind. The gentle kiss. His parting statement. Cullen remembered the process of coming out very well. First step, admitting to himself he might be gay but swearing to never act on it. Step two, acknowledging to himself he *was* gay but still vowing never to act on it. And lastly, getting to the point where he could no longer pretend. At that point, a guy could start to have seedy little trysts with strangers, or if he had the courage, actually come out. Worst case was seeing no way out and ending it all. Where was Abel in this process? He had apparently been through steps one and two, which would explain the endless praying for God to make him straight.

And then the kiss. Was he ready to come out, or was he at the point of no return? Being gay was not accepted in the Southern Baptist religion, least of all for the ministry, and that had been Abel's chosen career. If he came out now, he would have to give up his job and everything he believed in. Cullen knew what that felt like all too well. Was Abel strong enough to walk away from his job and the church? That was the real question. It all seemed so hopeless, but Cullen kept telling himself not to jump to conclusions. He knew firsthand how everything always seemed so much worse in the wee hours of the morning with no sleep and a load on your mind.

Resigned to the fact that sleep would remain unattainable for the remainder of the night, Cullen cursed under his breath as he got up to sit on the edge of the bed. The floor was cold against his bare feet. He sighed deeply, rubbed his eyes, and then rested his head in his hands. In his former life, in times like these, prayer had always comforted him, but not anymore. Cullen hadn't prayed since he'd held Cole's lifeless body in his lap and begged God to save the man he loved or to take him instead. But of course God hadn't listened, and Cullen was alone. That had been the end of his relationship with God. But at this moment of desperation, he was rethinking everything. After all, he wasn't asking for himself, only for Abel. The safety of a fellow man and new friend.

Oddly enough his body acted mostly on impulse, and he found his hands locked together in front of his chest. He looked up in disbelief and shook his head, not believing what he was about to do.

God, I'm a little out of practice. No, that's not true, I'm a lot out of practice, and you know damn well why. And just for the record, this is not about us. I'm putting my grievances with you aside this one time to ask for your help on behalf of a friend who is struggling. I hardly know this man, but what I do know about him tells me he is a good man and deserves to be happy. Just please keep him safe and bring him back home so I can try to help him. That's it, I guess. I don't hold out much hope, but this is my last option, and I have to give it a try.

Cullen got to his feet, and his first stop was the head. Exhausted, he felt like he was dragging a ton of lead behind him. Next stop was the galley. He leaned against the counter, arms across his chest as coffee brewed, the aroma slowly starting to stir his tired senses. The coffee pot beeped, signaling the brew was complete, and Cullen poured a cup and looked out of the galley porthole. Still pitch black. The clock revealed it was 5:30. *At least another hour before sunrise.*

Checking his cell phone again just to make sure he hadn't missed a call was an act of futility. The damn phone hadn't been out of his sight since he'd placed his first call to Abel. But Cullen did it just the same. *No missed calls. No voice mail.*

Cullen opened the companionway door and climbed the steps to the flybridge. The marina was eerily still. No wind. Not even a breeze. He instantly missed the familiar and comforting sounds of sailboat lanyards clanging against hollow aluminum masts. The only constant was the recurring flash of the Oak Island lighthouse, and the repeating glow steadied him somehow.

By sunrise, Cullen had finished off the entire pot of coffee. He was on a serious caffeine buzz, but at least he had a plan. His last and only hope of finding Abel. If this didn't work, Abel didn't want to be found, and Cullen felt he could leave Southport with a clear conscience. Not a fulfilled mission, but a clear conscience.

By seven forty-five, dressed in black slacks and a long-sleeved black dress shirt, Cullen stood in front of his mirror. *You look like an undertaker without your white collar.* But he'd long ago given up that attire.

Thirty minutes later he stood in front of Abel's house. He was disappointed when he didn't see a car in the driveway but hoped there was maybe a garage behind the house. He opened the gate, walked up the steps, and knocked. He waited. No one answered the door. Cullen knocked again, a little harder this time, and waited again. He listened closely, but there were no sounds or signs of life behind the front door.

Damn, Abel. Where are you?

His last hope was the Southport Baptist Church's administrative office. Cullen hoped the office would open by at least eight o'clock, but if not he'd sit there until it did open. Heading toward the church in his undertaker's outfit, Cullen felt bad because he knew he was going to be somewhat deceptive again. But his only chance of getting any information regarding Abel's whereabouts was to use the fellow reverend approach he'd used with Dottie and hope whoever he encountered took pity on him.

While Cullen walked he contemplated Abel's possible whereabouts. Maybe he was away on church business, but if that were the case, surely Abel would have mentioned that to him at some point. Or would he? They weren't really good friends. But what were they? What was the term some people used? *Two ships passing in the night.* But they hadn't missed each other. They'd actually met on a park bench. And yeah, they'd shared a couple of moments, but where did that leave them?

After Cullen nervously rounded the corner onto North Howe, he stopped and admired the church for a few minutes. Somehow it looked more regal now than it had the first time he'd seen it. But in all fairness, that had been at dusk, and this morning the bright sun was climbing in the sky, making the single steeple appear an extra vibrant white against the blue sky and deep red brick. The sun was even reflecting off of the highly polished bell in the bell tower, sending the sun's rays directly to the front door of the church like welcoming beams from heaven.

"Isn't that special?" Cullen mumbled sarcastically. "Listen to me. *Beams from heaven.* Like that would happen."

Cullen crossed North Howe and followed the signs around back to the church's office. A plaque outside the door said "Office Hours: Monday through Saturday, 8:00 a.m. to 5:00 p.m." Cullen knew it was well past eight, but he checked his watch anyway.

He took a deep breath and slowly pushed the door open. A little bell jingled, and a small voice said, "May I help you?"

Cullen's eyes hadn't yet adjusted, and he blinked into the dimly lit office. "I sure hope so." He smiled in the direction of the voice as an elderly lady standing behind a desk slowly came into view. She had silver-gray hair worn up in some sort of twist or bun. She was wearing a conservative cotton dress with a high collar, no noticeable makeup, and old-fashioned cat-eye glasses, turned up on each end and very pointy. Her smile was warm but guarded.

"Good morning," Cullen said. "I was wondering if Associate Pastor Weston was in this morning?"

"May I inquire as to who's asking?"

Cullen kept it short. "I'm Reverend Cullen Kiley from Massachusetts." *Best not to stretch the truth too much if I don't have to.* Cullen waited.

The woman tilted her head to one side and said nothing, apparently waiting for him to elaborate.

"Oh. I... I'm on vacation, passing through Southport on my boat, and was told by a mutual friend who also went to the seminary that Abel—I mean Associate Pastor Weston—was assigned here, so I just wanted to stop by and say hello."

The woman's smile was still hesitant. "Oh, I'm so sorry, Reverend, but Monday and Tuesday are Pastor Weston's days off. That boy works so hard. In fact, most times he doesn't even take his days off. But he left a message on the answering machine over the weekend saying he was going out of town unexpectedly and wouldn't be in until Wednesday."

Out of town! Not back until Wednesday? Cullen heard the words but couldn't believe them. He cursed internally but tried to offer some sort of response. "Oh, that's too bad."

"How long will you be in town?" the woman asked, sticking out her hand. "I'm Agnes Williams, by the way. My husband is the pastor here."

"Pleased to meet you, Mrs. Williams, but I'm not sure yet. If you hear from Abel, will you please tell him I stopped by and to please give me a call."

The woman slid a pad and pen across the desk, and Cullen jotted down his name and cell number and slid it back to her.

"I certainly will, Reverend"—she looked down at the pad—"Kiley."

Cullen knew Abel had his number, but Agnes did not, and Cullen didn't want to raise any suspicions for Abel's sake. He knew he was already taking a chance just by coming here.

"Thank you very much," Cullen said.

"You're very welcome. If Abel calls, rest assured he'll get your message."

"Thank you."

The woman came out from behind her desk, slid her arm in his, and walked him to the door. "Now you have a good day, Reverend," she said patting his forearm. "I hope you enjoy the rest of your stay in Southport."

Cullen nodded and smiled weakly. "Is the church open?" he asked, much to his surprise.

"As a matter of fact, it is. It's always open during regular business hours." Agnes lowered her head and looked at him over her glasses. "You know, when I was a little girl, it used to be open twenty-four hours a day for our congregation to stop in and pray anytime we felt the need. But as the years rolled on and people stopped respecting the church as God's house, it became necessary to lock the doors at night. I'd be happy to give you a tour if you like. Are you Southern Baptist, Reverend?"

Cullen responded without thinking. "No, ma'am. Episcopalian."

Like hell you are!

The woman nodded tightly but didn't respond.

Cullen laid his hand on top of Agnes's, which was still resting on his forearm. "Thank you again for your help, Mrs. Williams."

"My husband has told me on numerous occasions that we're different from Episcopalians, but in my book we are all God's children, so please feel free to visit our church and say a prayer for those in need."

"I think I'll do just that," Cullen said without conscious thought.

Closing the office door behind him, Cullen followed the path around to the front of the church, stopped, and looked up at the tall white steeple. He slipped his hands in his pockets and waited. He wanted to feel something. Anything that might give him a spark of the old flame he used to feel when he contemplated a place of worship. But nothing came.

Cullen walked up the steps, laid a hand on the shiny brass door handle, and slowly pulled the door open. Again it took a few minutes for his eyes to adjust to the dim light, but his ears instantly heard a song he recognized. He felt a stabbing pain in his heart, and his legs weakened to the point where he thought they just might crumple beneath him. He felt his way to the nearest pew and sat.

The song wasn't a hymn he'd ever heard or sung in the Episcopal Church, but one he'd heard from a spiritual country music CD Cole had purchased years ago simply to get a version of "Amazing Grace" by Martina McBride. The CD was a compilation of various country singers, and Kenny Chesney had done his version of the song now playing, "The Old Rugged Cross." It had become one of Cole's favorites and Cullen's as well. So much so that Cullen had it sung at Cole's memorial service.

Chill bumps covered the surface of Cullen's body, and the hair stood up on the back of his neck. *What are the odds?* As he sat there, he could feel the tears welling up. He closed his eyes tightly against the onslaught of emotions and bit his bottom lip hard enough that he was sure he'd drawn blood.

"How can any of this be happening?" Cullen said out loud.

I must be losing my mind. That's it. I'm finally going insane.

The vivid dreams. Abel. This church. This song. Why was Cole's memory so alive here?

How?

Why?

Cullen looked up again. *Have you not tortured me enough? What more do you want from me?*

Cullen listened in silence. With his eyes closed tightly, it was easy for him to imagine Cole sitting next to him, their hands joined as they enjoyed the simple melody and spiritual lyrics of the song. But when the song ended and Cullen opened his eyes, Cole wasn't there. And he was never going to be. Not ever. He closed his eyes again, willing the fantasy to come to life.

The church was silent for a few seconds. The next song started, and Cullen listened closely, half expecting Martina McBride to start her version of "Amazing Grace." But that miracle never came. The song that followed was one Cullen didn't recognize, and it held no difficult memories for him, for which he was very grateful. It allowed him to compose himself again and focus on the church and why he'd come. Why had he come? Was it to pray? Was it to curse God again? Why?

Cullen put those thoughts aside. He opened his eyes once again and studied the interior of the church. It wasn't nearly as grand as an Episcopal or Catholic church. There were no ornate columns or statues, and the altar was more of a lectern or pulpit with a single podium. Behind the pulpit, four or five steps led up to another level, quite possibly a choir loft. Behind the loft was a solid white wall with a four-sided wooden molding like a picture-frame encasing a substantial portion of it. The strange thing was there was nothing inside of the frame except a few fall-colored flowers in the lower corners. To the left and right of the frame was a ledge that ran horizontally to the end of the wall. The ledge was also covered with fall flowers. Oddly enough there was no depiction of Christ on the cross—or any visible crosses for that matter. No statue of Virgin Mary. No statue of Joseph.

In the places where these statues would historically be in his church, this one had a pit containing a guitar, a saxophone, and a set of drums instead, and directly across from it on the other side of the church, an organ pit. *So odd!*

Looking around further, Cullen noticed the entire church was carpeted in sapphire blue, and the pews were arranged in a semicircle. Also unlike his church, there were two separate aisles left and right of center instead of one aisle right down the middle. Cullen knew he was in a church, but it felt so different, so foreign. It was odd to not smell the familiar incense or hear the old pipe organ blaring out "The Lord's Prayer."

Then it suddenly dawned on Cullen that this was the first time he'd been in any kind of church since Cole's memorial service. All those memories descended upon him like the church itself had caved in. The memories of the music. The Word. The people. His inability to speak. Or feel. Cole's urn displayed prominently on the altar. The limo ride to the mausoleum with Cole's urn resting on his lap. The sound of rock on rock when the marble door slid closed on Cole's tomb. And then the emptiness of what used to be their home. His empty life now.

Cullen couldn't breathe. He grabbed the back of the pew in front of him with one hand and wrapped his other around his throat, gasping for air. He was hyperventilating, and luckily the survival instinct took over and he quickly lowered his head between his legs and concentrated on slowing his breathing. After a few minutes, when Cullen's breathing had returned to almost normal, he stood and walked to the back of the church.

Cullen froze with his hand on the door handle. *Way to go, Cullen. Does everything have to be about you? You didn't come here for you. Remember? Why else did you want to visit the sanctuary if not to ask again for help for Abel in God's house?*

Turning and staring straight ahead at the pulpit, Cullen whispered, "God, if you remember me at all, you must know how hard *this* is for me. How hard it is for me to be here. To ask you for anything. But *this* is not about me. I have come here and put our differences aside because I have a friend in need. In need of your help. He too has prayed for help and guidance and feels ignored by you. I have done everything I can to help, but as usual I've failed. He is a good man, so please bring him home and try to find it somewhere in your heart to help him."

Cullen turned and walked out of the church, down the steps, and onto the street. He'd done everything he'd known to do. The rest was up to the universe—or whatever higher power you believed in.

As Cullen walked along without direction, he found himself at the Riverwalk, strolling along the sidewalk. He stopped when he came to the bench he and Abel had shared a few days ago. He stared at it. Had it only been a few days? Cullen sat and gazed out over the water. The bright sunshine was now gone, the sky was a gray mass of gloomy clouds, and the water was leaden and rough. In the distance Cullen could hear rumbles of thunder, and suddenly people were scattering with a renewed sense of urgency in their step.

But Cullen didn't move. He allowed his mind to drift, mostly to second-guess his efforts. Had he exhausted every option to help Abel? Did Abel just want to be left alone? Did he need time to think? Agnes said Abel indicated he'd be back on Wednesday, so Cullen didn't think he'd do anything foolish. But he knew the man was in pain. And Cullen knew all too well that sometimes people in pain did foolish things. A chill ran down his spine.

A jagged streak of lightning split the sky just overhead, and Cullen jumped to his feet. At some point it had started raining, and he'd been so deep in thought, he'd not even noticed. He started back to the boat as the wind picked up. It began to rain harder; the thunder roared and the lightning danced over the water like Fourth of July fireworks.

When Cullen climbed back on *T-Time*, he was soaked to the bone. He stepped out of his shoes, shed his wet clothes, and peeled off his dripping socks. Down below, he stood under the spray of an extra-hot shower, but no matter how hot the water, Cullen just couldn't seem to get warm. When the water started to run cool, he shut it off, wrapped a towel around himself, and sat on the small bench in his shower. He rested his head against the shower wall and shivered. And shivered.

Finally getting up the nerve to venture outside of the stall, Cullen dressed in flannel pajama bottoms and a long-sleeved fleece pullover. Just as he stepped into his slippers, his cell phone beeped. *Oh no! Please, God, don't let me have missed a call from Abel.*

The screen read Missed Call and displayed Abel's number.

Cullen was about to hurl the phone across his cabin when he noticed there was a voice mail. He slid his trembling fingers across and tapped the screen a few times, and then he lifted the phone to his ear.

He gave a sigh of relief when he heard Abel's voice say, "Cullen."

But that relief quickly faded. "You went to my church, Cullen? What were you thinking, man? What did you tell them? Who did you say you are? How do we know each other? Oh my God, Cullen, did you tell Agnes you were gay? I could lose everything. I thought you were my friend."

The voice mail abruptly ended. Cullen dropped the phone and sat on the edge of his bed. His stomach was churning, and although he'd had nothing all day but coffee, he was in grave danger of losing whatever was in there. *How could Abel think I would do that to him?* It was as though Abel had reached into Cullen's chest and yanked his heart out. He lay back on the bed and closed his eyes. The rain pelted the hull of the boat, and the thunder and lightning rumbled and flashed, but Cullen was immune to it all. He felt, saw, and heard nothing as he lay motionless, staring blankly up at the ceiling of his cabin. And then his cell phone rang. Cullen scrambled to his feet and then dropped to his knees looking for his phone. When he found it, he saw Abel's number on the screen and answered. "Abel! I didn't do or say anything to hurt you. You didn't return any of my calls. I was worried about you."

Abel's voice cracked. "I'm so sorry."

No. Didn't crack. Abel was crying. "Abel, where are you? I'll get there as soon as I can."

"No," Abel said. "I'm so sorry, Cullen. I didn't mean.... I know you'd never do anything to intentionally hurt me."

"Abel, please," Cullen begged. "Just come back and we can talk all this through."

"No!" Abel said. "We can't be friends. You should probably go, Cullen. It's best for both of us."

"Abel! I know why you think we can't be friends."

Abel didn't respond.

"I've thought all along you were struggling with your sexuality, Abel. I remember the kiss. And I remember your words. 'We have more in common than you'd ever imagine.'"

"God, no!" Abel said. "I'm so sorry."

"Don't be," Cullen said. "It's okay, Abel. It's okay."

Abel's breathing was heavier, and Cullen could hear sobs. "No! It's not okay, and it will never be okay."

"I know it feels that way now, but it won't feel that way forever. I can get you through this, Abel. I promise you."

"I'm not gay. I don't want to be gay. I can't be gay," Abel yelled into the phone.

"Abel, just come back. We'll talk it through, and if you still want me to go, I'll leave tomorrow."

"No need," Abel said. "Nothing to talk through. Just please go, Cullen. It's the only way."

Cullen sighed. "This is not going away, Abel. It's not something you can cure. Me leaving won't change who and what you are."

"It might not cure me, Cullen, but it will take away this temptation I have to burn in hell. With you! Good-bye, Cullen."

Abel ended the call, and Cullen again sat on the bed. "Jesus! What have I done?"

CULLEN SAT in the dark saloon, the only light from a burning candle on the table in front of him and the intermittent flash of lightning strikes across the sky. The only sounds were from the rumbling thunder and the constant thumping of the waves against *T-Time*'s hull.

The power had gone off over an hour ago and instead of starting *T-Time*'s generator, he decided he liked the darkness and solitude. It fit his mood perfectly. Cullen was sipping his third shot of bourbon, and although nowhere near intoxicated, he found his sharp emotions had softened around the edges, and he was feeling more melancholy than anything else. The storm was showing no signs of calming, and in truth he found it all rather soothing.

What an appropriate way to spend my last night in Southport.

Late in the afternoon, he'd made up his mind to do as Abel had asked. He called the Charleston City Marina, reserved a slip for the rest of the winter, and told Southport Marina he was leaving tomorrow morning at first light.

It was the least he could do, but it was killing him to leave someone whom he now considered a friend at one of the darkest times of his life. And if he were being completely honest—this was probably the bourbon talking now—he felt an unlikely connection to Abel. That in itself was odd because he'd had no interest in new friends—or old friends for that matter—since Cole's death. *Why Abel?* Maybe it was simply because Cullen thought Abel needed him, and after so long, it felt good to be needed.

For some reason Cullen's dream came to mind, the one where Cole had handed him off to Abel and Abel had carried him to the surface. To live. And it was still nagging at him from somewhere just beyond conscious thought. When he forced himself to think about it now, his grief-counselor training kicked in and told him it was all more than likely nothing but his subconscious working overtime. So again he pushed it to the back of his mind and made no attempt to overanalyze. He wanted to simply dismiss it and let it go.

Cullen stared at the flickering candle, and his thoughts switched to Abel again. Leaving without saying good-bye or seeing Abel face-to-face was going to be difficult. He wanted to know that Abel was going to be all right, but that just wasn't in the cards. Although Cullen had taken Abel's earlier call very hard for a couple of hours, the more he thought about Abel's rage, the more he realized it was Abel simply reacting out of fear. The man was scared, paranoid, and oversensitive about his sexuality, pure and simple, and his emotions were doing the talking. Cullen thought he'd gotten to know Abel fairly well in the short time they'd had together, and he'd never heard Abel so much as raise his voice or speak ill of anyone or anything. No. It was definitely fear driving his anger. Abel had seemed to accept that Cullen would never reveal anything to the church about his suspicions, which had now been confirmed, but he still didn't want Cullen around. Would Abel regret that when he thought about it more rationally?

Then, as usual, his thoughts turned once more to Cole, who was the main reason Cullen was in Southport in the first place. Had Cole brought him and Abel together? Of course not. He no longer believed in fate or God's hand in making the world go around, but Cullen did realize he'd probably buried a few of his demons here, especially the fear that his memories of Cole were fading away to nothing. He still had a long way to go to get his life back on track, but holding on to Cole was not the way to do it. He would always have their memories, but he had to let the man himself go.

Holding his glass in the air, Cullen toasted the man he loved so desperately. "To you, my love. If there is a heaven, I'm sure you are there. But wherever you are, know when my time comes, I will find you. And hold you. And love you. I will always love you."

Cullen lowered his glass and downed the last of his bourbon. He held his empty glass in his hand and made no attempt to refill it or even move for that matter. He simply sat and listened to the storm raging all around him.

The sounds of the cracking thunder and the waves against the hull were so loud Cullen nearly missed the distinct thumps that sounded like someone knocking on *T-Time*'s hull. He jumped to his feet, opened the companionway door, and climbed the stairs to the cockpit. The silhouette of a man standing on the dock appeared against the cockpit's rain cover, hands frozen by his side, dripping wet and shivering. Cullen unzipped the vinyl curtain and there stood Abel. Soaked through and through.

Cullen ran to him, wrapped his arms around him tightly, and led him to the boat. When they reached the cockpit, Cullen once again zipped them in against the raging storm and turned. When their eyes met, Abel said, "Help me. I'm so tired of running."

CHAPTER NINE

ABEL WAS soaked, numbed, and chilled down to his core, but he felt safe and warm in Cullen's secure embrace. He heard Cullen's reassuring voice in his ear. "It's all going to be okay. I promise."

Cullen's voice was the only thing that saved him from breaking free and running. And running. And running. *No! I'm so tired of running. Isn't that what I said?*

Instead of running Abel tentatively brought his arms up, locked his hands behind Cullen's waist, and held on tight, not allowing himself the opportunity to flee. He buried his face in Cullen's neck and breathed for what seemed like the first time since Saturday night when he'd left this very boat.

After leaving Cullen, Abel had meandered through town and back to his church-owned house. He'd let himself in and walked through each empty room, listening to his steps echo through the bare halls. The house had once meant he'd finally had a place of his own. Much the same way he'd felt about the church. A home. But that had all changed when he realized he could no longer deny who and what he was. He'd tried for so long to block it out of his mind. He'd never acted on his desires and prayed to God day after day to take this burden from him, but his prayers were never answered. With each passing day, Abel had lost a little of himself until one man and one simple, stupid, innocent kiss had changed everything. One man and one kiss had breathed life back into Abel's mundane closeted life, but that same man and kiss had also charted a course for the future that could no longer be denied. Cullen was now just a reminder of what he could never have. What his church would never tolerate. What his congregation would try to pray out of him.

The realization had hit Abel hard. His choices? Fight or flee. And of course being the coward he was, he'd chosen to flee. His only hope was that Cullen would give up on him and simply leave Southport by the time Abel had to return. But he hadn't been prepared for the calls.

The desperate, repeated calls. The worry so obvious in the man's voice it had almost ripped Abel's heart out. And then he'd received the call from Agnes questioning him about a visit by an Episcopal priest named Reverend Cullen Kiley, who claimed to know him. He'd panicked then. What had Cullen told Agnes about their friendship? Abel had made up some cockamamie story about a mutual friend with whom he'd gone to the seminary. It had seemed to appease Agnes for the time being, but if she questioned him further, the story would not hold up. And Agnes wasn't the type to let anything go. Not much happened in Southport without her knowing about it, and she was very proud of that fact. And that's when he'd lost it and finally called Cullen. He wanted Cullen to go, and what better way to do it than to lash out at him. And it would probably have worked if Abel hadn't given in to his selfish needs and come back to Southport.

A flash of lightning brought Abel back to the moment. They both jumped. "Let's get down below," Cullen said.

Cullen led Abel downstairs, through the saloon, and into Cullen's cabin. He picked up a candle off of the table, the dancing flame illuminating their way through the darkness. Abel watched silently as the reflection of the flames danced on the cabin walls. When Cullen stopped in the doorway of the master head and turned to him, Abel wanted to move, but he was so cold, shivering so badly it was as if his limbs weren't working.

"We need to get you into some dry clothes." Cullen peeled Abel's jacket off and tossed it into the head, the weight of the soaked jacket making a thud when it hit the floor.

Abel couldn't remember ever being so cold. He stood frozen in place as Cullen pulled his T-shirt over his head, exposing Abel's bare chill-bump-covered chest. Cullen then dropped to his knees, and Abel lifted each foot as Cullen removed his sneakers and pulled off his wet socks.

It was as if he were no longer in control of his own body. Like he was outside of it somehow, watching the scene unfold in front of him. Cullen was on his feet again, unbuckling Abel's belt, releasing the button on his khaki pants, unzipping them, and peeling them off.

Cullen towel dried Abel's hair and body. "Don't move."

Cullen disappeared, and seconds later Abel felt a gentle vibration throughout the boat and heard a slight humming sound as the cabin lights came to life. Cullen returned, and Abel watched as he turned on the heat and then dug underwear, sweat pants, a sweatshirt, and a pair of socks out of several different drawers and then handed them to Abel. "Put these on." He pushed Abel into the head and closed the door behind him.

When Abel emerged from the head, now fully clothed and starting to feel his blood circulating again, Cullen was bare chested and pulling on a pair of pajama bottoms. He looked over his shoulder. "You okay?"

"No. And I don't think I'll ever be okay again," Abel said honestly.

Cullen walked over, again wrapped his solid arms around Abel, and held him tight. "You will," he whispered. "We'll figure this out."

This time there was no hesitancy in Abel's reaction. He lifted his arms and ran his hands across Cullen's smooth muscular back. "You're cold. You need a sweatshirt."

But Cullen didn't release him, and it took only a second for Abel to realize he liked the feel of Cullen's muscles under his hands. He gently kissed Cullen's neck. "You need clothing."

Cullen released him, reached into the head, and lifted a long-sleeved T-shirt from a hook on the back of the door. He pulled it over his head, took Abel by the hand, and led him to the saloon. "Sit. I'll make some coffee."

"I'd prefer some of that bourbon if you have it," Abel said shyly.

A reluctant smile tugged at Cullen's lips. "I knew giving you bourbon was a mistake. Are you sure?"

Abel nodded. "I'm sure. If I ever needed a drink, it's now."

Cullen poured two glasses of bourbon and led Abel to the couch. Cullen sat and crossed his legs under him, his foot brushing Abel's hand in the process. "My God, Cullen. Your foot is like a block of ice. Put your feet in my lap."

Cullen hesitated.

"Now!" Abel rubbed his hands together to warm them and then took Cullen's feet and rubbed them vigorously. They were both icy cold. After a few minutes, they felt a bit warmer to the touch, and Abel reached behind him and took a lap blanket off of the back of the couch and wrapped it tightly around Cullen. "There. That should keep you warm."

"Thank you," Cullen said eyeing Abel warily.

"I'm sorry," Abel finally said.

"For?"

Abel thought. *What am I sorry for?* "Everything," he said. "For running. For ignoring your calls and then blasting you when I did call you."

"Did you really think I would tell anyone at the church what I suspected? What good would that do either of us?"

Abel hung his head. "Honestly? No. I wanted you to leave Southport, and the only way I knew how to make that happen was to hurt you or make you angry enough to hate me."

"I could never hate you, Abel. But your idea worked. My plan was to pull out tomorrow morning."

Abel looked away. He didn't want Cullen to see the tears welling up in his eyes. But he had no one to blame but himself. After everything he'd done to make Cullen leave, did he have a right to ask him to stay?

Before Abel could answer his own question, Cullen slid his finger under Abel's chin and turned Abel's head until their eyes met. "I said my plan *was* to pull out tomorrow."

"You're not leaving?" Abel asked hesitantly, tears now flowing freely.

"Not now. Not unless you want me to."

"No! Please don't go."

Cullen brushed the tears away with his thumb. "But what's changed?"

"For starters," Abel said, "that kiss changed everything for me. After I kissed you, I knew I could never go back. But I was scared. I figured if you left Southport, the temptation would leave with you."

"What temptation?" Cullen asked.

But before Abel could answer the question, Cullen seemed to get it on his own. "Me?"

Abel nodded.

"Abel...," Cullen said, looking away. When he looked back, Cullen's usually brilliant blue eyes had gone flat. "I'm a dysfunctional mess who can't move on with his life because he's still mourning the loss of his husband almost two years later. What do I have to offer you but misery?"

"That's just it," Abel said, taking Cullen's hand in his. He wasn't sure if it was the bourbon or what, but he was feeling more confident in his convictions. "I'm a closeted gay Southern Baptist minister who's never even been with another man. What do I have to offer *you* but misery? But yet I came back. And... you're still here."

Cullen didn't respond.

It has to be the bourbon, but at this very moment, I don't care. Abel leaned forward and pressed his lips lightly against Cullen's, and they were just as warm and soft as he'd remembered. When Cullen didn't pull away, Abel ran his tongue along Cullen's lips. Cullen opened slightly, and Abel pushed his tongue inside, kissing Cullen deeply and passionately. Abel had kissed girls on dates in high school, mostly because he had to, but this.... This was a real kiss. Blood was pumping through his veins at breakneck speed and chill bumps were forming all over his skin. It was like nothing he'd ever experienced. He reached his hand behind Cullen's head and pulled him in closer. He needed him closer. Abel found a new sense of courage and acted on it. His tongue explored Cullen's mouth, tasting the sweetness of the bourbon mixed with Cullen's own sweetness. Abel was losing himself in the kiss when suddenly Cullen withdrew.

"I'm sorry. I'm not ready for this," said Cullen.

At first the rejection was like a jab to the heart, but Abel remembered Cullen and Cole's story. He knew Cullen was struggling, and maybe, just maybe, they could help each other move on. "I understand," Abel said. "I shouldn't have done that. I'm sorry."

"It's not you," Cullen said quickly, taking Abel's hand. "It's just...."

"I know," Abel said. "It's Cole."

Cullen didn't respond, but he didn't need to. From the look of pain on his face, Abel already knew he was right.

Cullen took a sip of his bourbon and looked at Abel. "I'm sorry."

"Please don't apologize," Abel said. "I've been in the foster care system all my life, and I've had enough 'I'm sorry' to last a lifetime. 'I'm sorry your mother didn't want you.' 'I'm sorry no one adopted you.' 'I'm sorry this foster home isn't going to work out.' 'I'm sorry those people hit you.' 'I'm sorry you aged out of the system.' You see, Cullen, I'm done with apologies. I've had way more than my share."

To his credit, Cullen said nothing, but seconds later Abel once again found himself wrapped in Cullen's embrace. Abel closed his eyes and melted into Cullen's secure hold. *Being in Cullen's arms must be what it feels like to have a real home. To really belong somewhere.*

"It feels good to be held," Abel said. "So safe and secure. Something I never had growing up."

"It does feel good," Cullen said. "It's been so long for me, I'd almost forgotten."

Abel nuzzled down against Cullen's body and rested his head on Cullen's chest. "Can I share something with you?"

"Sure," Cullen said.

"This is a first for me."

"What's a first?"

"Being held like this," Abel clarified.

"You've never been held?"

"Not really," Abel said. "My foster parents were mostly in it for the money. I mean… they'd kiss me on the top of my head and squeeze my shoulders every now and then when the social worker came around, but other than that, I was nothing more than a paycheck. I had a roof over my head and food in my stomach, and at the time I thought that was more than I deserved."

Cullen sighed and tightened his grip on Abel.

Abel raised his head. "Don't get me wrong. I learned much later when I became a pastor that there are some wonderful foster families out there. Unfortunately, those families weren't in the cards for me. I never saw any of them until I'd aged out of the system."

"I'm so sor—" Cullen stopped midsentence. "I almost apologized again."

"I know. It's okay."

"That must have sucked."

"The good thing is, you can't miss what you never had," Abel said. "But now that I've had it, you've ruined me for the rest of my life."

Cullen squeezed him a little tighter. "You're a wonderful man, Abel. Now that you're embracing your true self and beginning to live the life you're meant to live, you're gonna find more love than you ever imagined."

Abel didn't know what to say. And then he thought about the church. "You know, at one time I thought the church and God was what it felt like to have a home. And over the years, both have given me a sense of belonging that I'd not experienced growing up, but looking back now, it never really felt real. Secure."

"Maybe because you were using the church as something to hide behind."

"What do you mean?" Abel asked. "Are you saying my faith isn't real?"

"No. That's not it at all," Cullen said. "But you joined a religion that you knew was not accepting of homosexuality and spent the better part of your adult life praying to be straight."

"That's true," Abel agreed. "I knew at a very young age I was different. And when I reached puberty, I knew what being different meant. The only problem was, I was never secure enough in my life to share it with anyone. I always thought if I told one of my foster parents I was gay, they would just send me back. I didn't have the best of homes, but at least I had one. So I turned to my faith. I read the Bible and prayed for God to save me."

"Oh, Abel," Cullen said. Abel detected the crack in his voice. Cullen waited a few minutes and then spoke again. "None of this means your faith in God is any less real. It got you through some pretty rough times, and to me that's what faith is. Believing in something you can't see or touch. Something that gives you hope. In the short time I've known you, I believe you have the calling and the temperament to be a wonderful spiritual leader. You just have to find the right church."

"Thank you. And what about you, Cullen? Have you completely lost your faith?"

Cullen was silent for a long time. When he finally spoke, his voice was low. "I don't know. A few days ago I would have said yes, but this morning I was so worried about you, I put my differences with God aside and went to your church and prayed that he would bring you home and take care of you."

Surprised and touched, Abel lifted his head. "Cullen! No one has ever made a sacrifice like that for me. I know how hard that must have been for you."

"I had no choice. I was leaving in the morning. It was my last resort and… well, my prayer was answered."

Abel sat up, took Cullen's hand in his, and looked him directly in the eyes. "I can't help but think God had a hand in our meeting. We were two complete strangers, both at crossroads in our lives. Do you really think our paths crossed by accident?"

"I don't know what to think anymore," Cullen said.

"Do you mind if I lay my head on your chest again?"

Cullen opened his arms, and Abel snuggled back against him. Cullen tightened his grip on Abel, and they lay there in silence for the longest time.

Abel broke the quiet. "You already know I prayed day after day for God to take this burden from me. But after meeting you, someone who was also in the clergy in a religion that accepts everyone, I began to think. Maybe God *did* make me this way. I may no longer fit into my current church, but there are other ways to serve God and still stay true to oneself. Aren't there?"

"Of course there are," Cullen said.

"I'm not foolish enough to think that it's gonna be all smooth sailing from here on out," Abel said. "But at least I'm taking the first step and heading down the right path."

"You're right. You're gonna have to make some tough decisions regarding the church and the direction to take your life," Cullen added.

"I know," Abel said. "But I'm through running. I've already decided to resign my position with the church, but what I haven't decided is how to do it. Do I stand tall and give them an explanation, or do I take the easy way out and simply resign with no explanation?"

"That's gonna have to be your decision, but in my opinion, you owe them nothing."

"Thank you for listening, Cullen. I've never had a friend I could talk to like this. You can't know how much this means to me."

ANOTHER HOUR or so passed with little to no conversation. Cullen felt content and comfortable snuggled against Abel's warm body, and although Abel seemed to be in his own head, he also seemed contented and relaxed.

Abel raised his head. "Listen."

Cullen cocked his head to one side and listened. Nothing but the smooth humming of the generator. "The storm's passed."

Lifting up just a little, Cullen looked out of the window. The power was on and the marina was once again all aglow. "I guess I should switch back to shore power and give the generator a rest."

"Does that mean I have to get up?" Abel asked.

Cullen chuckled. "I'm afraid so."

Abel slid off of Cullen, straightened, and sat on the end of the couch. "What time is it anyway?"

Cullen looked at the clock on the microwave oven. "Just after one o'clock."

"Wow! I didn't realize it was so late. I should let you get some rest."

"It's been an enlightening day for both of us," Cullen said.

"That's an understatement." Abel looked around for his shoes, dreading putting his warm, dry feet back in those wet, cold sneakers.

"Stay," Cullen said, shocking himself. *What the hell?*

Abel looked surprised but shook his head. "No. I couldn't. I don't want to impose."

Cullen waved him off. "Your sneakers are soaked, as are all of your clothes, and although you're welcome to what you have on, I don't think my shoes will fit you."

Abel looked like he was trying to decide if this was a good idea or not.

"Aren't you off tomorrow?" Cullen added before Abel could respond.

"Yeah—wait. How do you know that?" Abel paused. "On second thought, let me guess. Agnes?"

Cullen nodded.

Abel's smile was wry. "I swear that woman has a mouth as big as the Atlantic."

"So. It's settled. You'll stay."

Abel still looked hesitant, but he nodded.

Cullen opened a cabinet door and flipped a switch, and the hum of the generator slowly disappeared. "You ready for bed?"

"Yeah," Abel said. "It's been a long, emotional day. Where do you want me to sleep?"

Cullen studied Abel's face for some sort of indication of what he wanted, but Abel's expression was unreadable.

Did he want Abel in his bed? The same bed he'd shared with Cole? It wasn't sex. It was just sleeping, but still, that was almost as intimate.

And if he did want Abel in his bed, he didn't want to be presumptuous and assume Abel wanted to be there.

But Abel had surprised him tonight. It was heartbreaking to think that Abel had been starved of any real affection, security, and warmth, and tonight his need for human touch seemed to be insatiable. He would do it. He would do it for Abel.

"Would you like to sleep with me?" Cullen asked cautiously.

"Again, I don't want to impose," Abel said. "I know this boat was yours and Cole's. Would that be too weird for you? I can leave. Really."

"No, I want you to stay." And Cullen realized he did want Abel to stay. Not just for Abel, but for himself as well. It had been a long time since he'd held someone, and it had felt good. "It might be weird at first, but I need to get past these types of hurdles if I'm ever going to move on with my life. But only if you want to."

Abel offered Cullen a feeble smile. "I would like that. For some reason the thought of being alone tonight seems almost unbearable."

"Then it's settled. Can I get you anything before we turn in?"

"I'm good."

Abel stood motionless as Cullen walked around turning off the lights in the cabin. When Cullen was through, he grabbed two bottles of water from the galley and looked at Abel. It was as though the man couldn't move his feet.

"It's okay," Cullen said walking over, taking Abel by the hand, and leading him down below.

"Which is your side?" Abel asked apprehensively when they reached the cabin.

"The right," Cullen said tossing one of the water bottles to Abel.

Abel caught the bottle and placed it on the bedside table. "Good. I'm a lefty."

Cullen brushed his teeth and returned to the cabin, where he found Abel sitting on the edge of the bed. "I left a new toothbrush on the counter for you if you want it."

"Thanks." When Abel reached the door to the head, he stopped and turned. "Thank you, Cullen. No one… has ever been this kind to me."

Without waiting for a response, Abel disappeared into the head and closed the door behind him.

Cullen swallowed the lump in his throat and fought back the tears that were welling up in the backs of his eyes. He couldn't imagine what it must have been like for Abel growing up with no one who truly loved him. No one to talk to. No one to hold him when he was scared or sick. No wonder he turned to religion. God must have seemed like his only friend. Cullen looked up to the heavens, and for the first time in a very long time, he didn't curse the Almighty but silently thanked him for bringing Abel back and for being there for Abel all those years.

Cullen pulled back the blankets, removed his shirt and pajama bottoms, and crawled into bed. He leaned against the headboard, fingers linked behind his head. Abel reappeared with his sweatshirt in hand. It had been dark when Cullen had stripped Abel's wet clothing off earlier, and he'd been too worried to do anything but get Abel dry and warm. But now, in the light of the cabin, he could clearly see Abel's well-defined pectorals, taut nipples, and yes, count 'em. One. Two. Three. Four. Five. Six pack. His upper arms were almost as big around as Cullen's thighs. *Damn, the man is ripped.*

Abel walked around the bed, and Cullen pulled back the covers as an invitation. "Work out much?" he teased.

Even in the softly lit cabin, Cullen could see the blush creeping into Abel's face. "A little." Abel turned his head away shyly. "It's my only guilty pleasure."

Abel stood motionless, almost like he was trying to make some sort of decision, and then he scanned the room. He appeared to stop when he saw Cullen's pajama bottoms on the floor next to the bed, slipped off his own sweats, peeled off his socks, and finally slid into bed.

Cullen could feel Abel trembling and didn't know if Abel was cold or nervous, so he wrapped an arm around him and pulled him close. Abel quickly laid his head on Cullen's chest, as he had on the couch, and sighed heavily.

"You okay?" Cullen asked.

"Yeah. Just a little nervous, I guess. You're the first person I've shared a bed with since I was a kid in foster care."

Cullen laughed and gave Abel a quick squeeze. "Why? Do you snore?"

Abel appeared to be seriously contemplating the question, and Cullen couldn't hold back a chuckle. Abel must have realized he was teasing and smacked Cullen playfully on the arm. "No. I don't snore, thank you very much. Do you?"

"Nope," Cullen said. "I'm a fairly quiet sleeper. I turn a few times. Get up to pee once or twice, but other than that, I'm a great bedmate."

"I guess I'll be the judge of that." Abel snuggled closer, and Cullen shivered as Abel's close-cut beard brushed over his bare skin. Abel rested his hand on Cullen's stomach and then slowly moved it up and over Cullen's chest. He brushed Cullen's nipple gently before following the little path of hair that ran down Cullen's chest to his belly button and disappeared into the waistband of his underwear. When he was finished, he repeated the process all over again. Abel was almost childlike in his exploration, and Cullen was surprisingly comfortable indulging him. After all, Abel had suppressed his desires for so many years. That was the least he could do.

Cullen closed his eyes and allowed himself to enjoy the sensation of Abel's soft touch. Little pangs of guilt kept trying to intrude on his pleasure, but he pushed them to the far reaches of his mind. He would deal with them, but not tonight. Tonight appeared to be a night of firsts—obvious firsts for Abel, but equally as important, firsts for Cullen as well.

For starters, there had never been another man in this bed but Cole, and that was a tough one to acknowledge. Not as hard as the realization that Cullen had not been this relaxed and open with anyone since Cole, though, nor had anyone touched him this way. Lying here now with Abel in his arms left him with nothing but unprotected honesty, and the feeling scared the hell out of him. Abel seemed to have this ability to strip away Cullen's defenses, one by one, but Cullen couldn't or wouldn't let it go any further than simple touch. On the other hand, Cullen was surprised at himself for allowing it to happen at all. And he did not regret a single moment of it. Yet.

The sounds of the water lapping against the hull and the gentle rocking of the boat, combined with Abel's caresses, quickly lured Cullen into a deep sleep.

A storm was raging outside. Lightning was cracking in between roars of thunder. Cullen kept hearing his name over and over, like someone was calling him from far, far away. He looked out of windows but saw no one. Again he heard his name. Closer. Louder. He again looked out of the port-side windows. Nothing. He ran to starboard. Still nothing.

Then he heard his name again. This time louder and more desperate. "Cullen! Help me!"

Cullen ran down the steps to his cabin and peered out of the large porthole facing aft. The marina was in darkness, and the rain was pelting so hard against the window it was difficult to see anything. And then a bright flash of lightning illuminated a figure standing behind the boat, his arms stretched out, face pale and lifeless. Cole! The lightning flashed again. No, wait! That's not Cole. It's Abel.

Cullen ran up to the cockpit, peeled back the vinyl and canvas, and almost fell backward when the wind and pelting rain assaulted him. He covered his face, brushed the rain from his eyes, and blinked. Abel was still standing there, arms open, beckoning him. Cullen fought the wind and made his way down the back stairs to the dock. The lightning flashed again, and Abel's eyes looked dark and lifeless. He wrapped his arms around Abel and pulled him close. And then over Abel's shoulder, he saw him. Cole was standing on the dock behind Abel, seemingly unaffected by the wind and the rain. He was smiling affectionately. Cullen immediately let go of Abel and ran down the dock to Cole, throwing his arms around him. Cole returned the embrace, and Cullen began to cry. He was home. Cole had come to take him wherever he was going. Relief filled his entire being, and his heart was overcome with joy.

Cole placed both his hands on Cullen's shoulders and stepped away from the embrace. He was smiling, and his eyes were warm and full of love. He leaned in and pressed his lips against Cullen's. Cole's lips were soft and oh so familiar, but as soon as their lips met, a thousand memories flashed through Cullen's mind. Him and Cole side by side at the helm of T-time. *The two of them laughing hysterically as Cullen's chair collapsed on the beach in P-town. Each lost in the other's eyes on the day of their wedding. Cole in the first row of the church staring up at Cullen with so much love Cullen's heart hurt. Watching the fireworks here in Southport on the deck of* T-Time. *All their vacations together. Everyday life. And then Cole pushed his tongue into Cullen's mouth, kissing him so deeply, so wholly, that spots swam in front of Cullen's eyes. Cullen was elated and leaned into the kiss, giving himself to Cole. When the kiss ended, Cullen rested his forehead against Cole's and sighed.*

"I've missed you so much. I'm ready."

Cole gave Cullen a reassuring smile and offered his hand. Cullen gladly accepted it and allowed Cole to lead him down the dock. Cullen was happy for the first time since Cole's death. Really happy. Until he saw Abel standing where Cullen had left him, still being pelted by the raging storm. He looked lost, and his face was consumed with sadness. Oh my God. He'd forgotten all about Abel. His friend. Someone who needed him. Guilt consumed Cullen as he wondered how many times in Abel's life people had forgotten about him. He was suddenly no better than anyone else who'd abandoned Abel in the past. He was full of shame and regret.

Cullen realized he was suddenly struggling with a decision. Stay with Abel or go with Cole. To be with Cole again was all Cullen had wanted, dreamed of, since Cole's passing, and now the fact that he was even considering staying with Abel confused him deeply.

Cole led Cullen to Abel, released Cullen's hand, and joined it with Abel's. The minute his and Abel's hands touched, the storm quieted and the stars appeared shining brightly in the indigo night sky.

"No," Cullen whispered.

Cole looked at them both, and his expression conveyed nothing but love, peace, and happiness. "We shared a lifetime," Cole said as all their years of happiness again flashed behind Cullen's eyes. "It's time for us both to move on."

Cullen quickly realized the decision to go or stay had never really been his. Cole hadn't come to take him away; he'd come to make sure he and Abel found their way to each other.

Cole turned and started walking away. When Cullen called out to him, Cole stopped and looked over his shoulder. His smile was angelic, and although Cullen didn't see Cole's mouth move, he heard Cole's voice very clearly in his head. "Be happy, my love."

Cullen watched the man he so desperately loved slowly walk away from him. As Cole moved farther and farther away, a warm light began to encircle him. Cullen's heart broke in two as Cole looked back one more time, smiled, and then simply faded away.

The moment Cole disappeared, the pain in Cullen's aching heart was replaced with hope and promise. Cullen looked at Abel, and suddenly it all made sense.

CHAPTER TEN

ABEL WOKE slowly. The tight grip of slumber just didn't seem ready to release him, and he decided he was okay with that. Most mornings, probably as a result of living in so many different foster homes, he woke very disoriented. But this morning he knew exactly where he was: safe, warm, and comfortable in Cullen's bed. Abel unconsciously reached over for Cullen, and when he felt only cool sheets, he quickly opened his eyes and scanned the room. Cullen was nowhere in sight. Abel rolled over onto his back, listened closely, and sighed with relief when he heard the faint sounds of pots and pans and Cullen moving around elsewhere in the boat, probably the kitchen. *No, Abel. Galley. Not kitchen.*

Abel rolled over onto his side, nuzzled back into the warm bedding, and buried his head in Cullen's pillow. He inhaled deeply, and Cullen's scent filled his nostrils.

Closing his eyes, Abel remembered the extraordinary feeling he'd had last night of falling asleep in someone's arms for the first time ever. For over an hour, he'd rubbed Cullen's chest and abdomen, lightly tracing the little line of hair that led down to his navel, curved into a circle and then continued farther, hinting at what was below, before disappearing into Cullen's underwear. For some reason, he'd thought if he'd stopped touching and caressing Cullen, it might all turn out to be a dream, and when he woke, he'd be alone again. But he'd woken up several times during the night, and Cullen had still been there, holding him. He'd simply tightened his grip on Cullen and fallen immediately back to sleep.

Suddenly the aroma of bacon drifted into the cabin, and Abel's nose perked up. He couldn't remember the last time he'd eaten, and he was starved. He decided he would join Cullen and see if he could help. Pulling the covers back to get up, he heard Cullen's voice.

"No, sir. Back in bed."

Abel looked up to find Cullen standing in the doorway, smiling and holding a tray of breakfast.

"I thought I might help with breakfast."

Cullen walked into the room. "Got it all under control."

After putting the tray on the end of the bed, Cullen fluffed Abel's pillow. "Now lean back and let me do something nice for you." Cullen placed the tray in front of Abel. "I hope you like your eggs over easy?"

"Any way is fine by me. But what about you?"

Cullen turned. "I'll be right back."

Minutes later Cullen returned with another tray loaded with more breakfast. Abel lifted the covers, and Cullen climbed back into bed and rested the tray on his lap.

"This was really nice of you," Abel said.

"Please tell me you've had breakfast in bed before?" Cullen asked with an expression of hope plastered on his face.

"Yep. Once. When I was in the hospital getting my appendix removed, they brought me breakfast in bed. But I can guarantee it wasn't as good as this is going to be."

"Oh jeez, Abel. What am I going to do with you?"

Abel wanted to say, "You can do anything you want to me as long as you don't leave me." But of course he bit his tongue. He'd stopped asking for such foolishness a long time ago. *People leave, Abel. Or they send you away. That's just what they do.*

Abel couldn't help but recall one of his earliest childhood memories of clinging to a woman he'd thought was his mother when he was once again being reassigned in the foster care system.

Cullen interrupted his musings. "A penny for your thoughts."

"I don't think you realize what you're asking," Abel replied. "There's a lot of crazy in this head."

Cullen put his fork down and took Abel's hand. "You looked like you were miles away and had the saddest expression on your face. If you don't want to share, I understand."

Abel bit his bottom lip, trying to decide what to tell Cullen. He didn't want to lie, but he also didn't want Cullen thinking he was some sort of whiny baby. *Poor, poor me. I've had such a bad life.*

In the end he decided on the truth. The truth was, he'd had a shitty life. He wasn't whining about it. It was just a fact. He sighed. "I was just remembering how hard it was to understand why I didn't have a family of my own. Or why I kept going from one home to another. I'd always try to be good and do everything asked of me, but something always happened, and when it did, I was the first thing to go."

Cullen was silent for a while, like he was processing what Abel had said, and then he squeezed Abel's hand. "I can't imagine what that must have been like. Can I ask what triggered that memory?"

Abel looked away. *Now I'm really screwed.* But again Abel didn't want to lie. "You're gonna think it's ridiculous, and I'm embarrassed to tell you, but I can't lie."

"Why don't you let me decide if it's ridiculous or not."

"If you insist," Abel said. He hesitated.

"Well?"

"Man, you are a tenacious one."

"I'm still waiting."

Abel swallowed hard. "Okay. A minute ago when you teasingly asked what you were gonna do with me? My first thought was to say you can do anything you want to me—but just don't leave. I'm sorry, it was a gut reaction. In my world leaving is what people have always done, but I knew it wasn't fair to ask that of you, so I didn't say anything. And then some old childhood wounds started to resurface."

Cullen didn't respond, and Abel mentally kicked himself.

"See, I told you it was crazy." Anything to break the silence.

Cullen turned to face him. "First of all it's not ridiculous. And secondly you are right. It's not fair to ask that of me. And even if you did, I can't in good conscience make a promise I'm not sure I can keep. You know better than anyone that I'm struggling with my own demons."

"I know," Abel whispered. "I should have just kept my mouth shut."

Cullen held up a finger. "But what I can promise is that as long as I'm here, I'll do everything to get you through this rough patch."

Abel laughed. "Rough patch?"

"Yeah. Rough patch," Cullen said. "Abel. This uncertainty and fear isn't going to last forever. You're gonna be a great homosexual in no time at all."

Cullen's voice was warm. There was a smile hiding behind his comforting words, mixed with a little amusement, and it warmed Abel.

"I'll just have to take your word for it."

"THAT HIT the spot." Abel folded his napkin and placed it on his breakfast tray. He slid the tray down to his feet and pulled the covers back. "I'll do the dishes."

"Nope." Cullen held up his tray, swung his feet to the side of the bed, and stood. "I made the mess, I'll clean the dishes."

"Then we'll do them together." Abel stood too, not taking no for an answer.

"Okay, you win, but it's gonna be a tight squeeze in the small galley."

"I'm a foster kid, remember?" Abel laughed, following Cullen up the stairs to the galley. "I'm used to tight spaces. Hey! Once my bedroom consisted of simply a mattress in a closet."

"Seriously?" Cullen asked. "Didn't they have social workers that checked up on this sort of thing?"

"Absolutely. But they were all spread too thin, and when they finally got around to checking in on me, they saw where I was sleeping, and off I went to a new home. But at least I had a space of my own." Abel stopped when he realized what he'd said. "Man, I was even in the closet as a kid."

Cullen chuckled as they worked together effortlessly in the small space. When Cullen zigged, Abel zagged, and vice versa, each man dancing around the other.

Cullen threw a dishtowel over his shoulder and rested his hands on his hips. "You're pretty good at the galley dance. As I said before, Cole was the only other person who could pull it off."

"Thank you. I'll take that as a compliment. At least I'm in good company."

"Ya know," Cullen said, "that's the first time I've mentioned Cole and not felt a stab of loneliness and pain."

Abel smiled. "Maybe we're both making progress."

"I think so," Cullen said. "Hey! How about a run?"

Abel turned quickly in the little space, and the two men ended up face-to-face, chest touching chest. Crotch against crotch. Their eyes locked as they held each other's gaze. Abel was instantly lost in Cullen's beautiful blue eyes, and Cullen seemed to be lost in his. Abel raised his hands, cupped Cullen's face, and pressed his lips to Cullen's. The comfort with which he did it surprised him.

Not only did Cullen not pull away, he gripped Abel by the waist and pulled him closer. Abel took that as encouragement and timidly pushed his tongue inside Cullen's mouth. Cullen was warm, and he tasted of eggs and coffee, and it was overwhelmingly divine. Cullen gripped the back of Abel's neck with one hand, and the simple touch made Abel realize he was very hungry for something more. Something he'd never experienced. He knew then he wanted Cullen, no two ways about it.

But an internal struggle had started to manifest itself. Abel now knew what he wanted, but he also knew Cullen was still struggling with Cole's death. He needed to slow this down or Cullen was going to freak. Abel was about to retreat when Cullen beat him to it.

"No. I can't," Cullen said breathlessly into Abel's mouth, but to Abel's surprise, Cullen didn't release his hold on him. "I… it's not you. I'm screwed up, Abel. Until I met you, being miserable and alone had become an accepted way of life for me."

"And now?" Abel asked cautiously.

Cullen looked down and then looked back up to meet Abel's gaze. "It's like… I'm on this emotional rollercoaster. There's you. There's Cole's memory. And there's all the ups and downs that go with both. I just need more time to figure this all out. Okay?"

Abel rested his forehead against Cullen's and closed his eyes. "Okay."

Gently, Abel stroked Cullen's back, trying to comfort him in any way he could, and when Abel opened his eyes again, Cullen was staring back at him with an expression of absolute confusion. It broke Abel's heart to see Cullen so confused and in so much pain.

Abel took a deep breath and spoke slowly, willing his voice to sound steady and sure. "I really like you, Cullen, and although I know you're still struggling with your memories of Cole, I just want you to know I want you, if and when you are ever ready. No pressure, and

I'll let you take the lead, but I wanted you to know. To hear the words from my lips."

"Thank you," Cullen said. "One minute I don't think I'll ever be ready, and then I keep having these weird dreams that make me hopeful I can work through this. And then... well. This happens."

"It's okay, Cullen. Forget about what just happened between us. Would you like to tell me about the dreams? Sometimes it helps to talk about them."

Cullen hesitated and then took Abel by the hand. "Let's sit down."

When they were comfortably seated in the saloon, Cullen recounted his dreams, obviously struggling to give Abel as much detail as he could. Abel listened without interruption and tried to analyze as they went. Pastoral counseling training didn't make him a psychologist, but he had learned to listen with his heart. When Cullen was done, Abel chose his words carefully.

"As much as I want to, I hesitate to comment," Abel said.

"Why? I want your opinion."

"But after listening as objectively as I could, I'm afraid everything I say is going to sound like I'm trying to convince you to do something you might not want to do."

"I trust you, Abel. You're not a selfish man. I want to hear what you have to say."

Abel turned away, trying to decide how to proceed, but there was no real decision to be made. He had to give Cullen his opinion without sugarcoating it, whether he liked it or not. "Okay, but this is my take. You probably won't agree, but here's what I think."

Cullen took Abel's hand in his. "Remember, I trust you. It's okay."

"Well, for starters I think the dreams are telling you that Cole has not moved on because you haven't moved on. In the first dream, he leads you into the water and tries to show you that you're drowning, going deeper and deeper into yourself. And then he hands you off to me. Someone who pulls you to the surface and gives you air. Gives you life. He wants you to live, Cullen. Not only to live but be happy."

Cullen didn't respond, so Abel kept going. "In the second dream, he also brings you to me. He tells you he loves you, but it's time for you both to move on. He puts your hand in mine and disappears into the light. If he is willing to go into the light, he knows you're in good hands with me. Don't you see, Cullen? God, the universe, whatever you believe in, brought you to me. Because I needed you. But more importantly because you needed me. We needed each other."

Abel brought Cullen's hand to his lips and kissed it gently. "That's my take. Like it or leave it. And call it selfish or self-serving, call it me wanting you, call it whatever you want, but in my heart of hearts, that's what I believe."

Cullen took Abel into his arms. "I want to believe Cole was helping me. Guiding me. But what if all this is just my subconscious trying to justify my moving on?"

"The way I see it, it doesn't matter who or what's behind it. Something is telling you that you can't go on living the way you have been. From what you've told me, I think you've been slowly dying inside. And, Cullen, the body instinctively wants to survive. Somewhere deep down, whether you know it or not, you *want* to survive. I'm sure of it."

"I just need time to process all this."

"Of course you do," Abel said. "And take all the time you need. I'm not going anywhere."

"Thank you."

A couple minutes of silence passed and Cullen smiled weakly. "You still in the mood for that run?"

"Sure. But can we go by my house first so I can change?"

ABEL STOPPED dead in his tracks when he saw his house from across the street.

"What's wrong?" Cullen asked.

"Look!" Abel pointed. His house was totally decorated for the fall season. There was a huge corncob wreath with orange and gold leaves adorning the front door. Pumpkins in various sizes were lined up on the porch, and a cornstalk garland ran from one end of the white picket fence to the other.

"It's not bad," Cullen said, trying to sound convincing.

"It looks like Disneyland."

"Who did this?" Cullen asked.

"The ladies of the church," he said, wincing. "They do this for every holiday."

"Did they skip Halloween?"

"That's a very touchy subject at our church. The Southern Baptists are divided on whether to celebrate Halloween or not. Some allow their children to dress up and trick-or-treat, and some think it's the demon's holiday and lock their door and turn off all their lights. It all goes back to paganism and the rituals that go with it. And since the congregation is divided, the church sort of ignores the holiday altogether."

"Wow!" was all Cullen could say.

"Abel! You're back." Abel's neighbor Dottie waved from a rocking chair on her front porch.

"Yes, ma'am." Abel and Cullen crossed the street and stopped just outside her fence.

"Hello, Reverend Kiley. I'm so glad you boys didn't miss each other."

Abel raised one eyebrow and gave Cullen a quizzical stare.

"Long story," Cullen said, feeling a blush creep up his face. "Good to see you again, Mrs. Arnold."

"Another long story?" Abel teased through clenched teeth.

"Sorry."

Dottie gestured toward Abel's house. "Looks like the church monkeys paid you a visit again, Abel."

"Looks like," Abel replied, obviously trying to hide his disapproval.

"They mean well," Dottie said.

"I know, Dottie. I know. It's good to see you. The *reverend* and I"—Abel glanced at Cullen, and Cullen thought he detected a little sarcasm in his voice—"are gonna go for a run, so I need to get changed."

Abel slid the key in his lock and pushed the door open. When they were safely inside, he turned to Cullen. "Anything you want to tell me?"

This time Cullen felt the heat that accompanied the blush as it crept up his face. "Okay. I'm sorry. I was desperate to find you. I didn't know where you lived, and I didn't have your cell number, and I was running out of time. Then I remembered you told me you lived a few blocks from the marina, so I ran up and down every street within a five-block radius, hoping I'd see you in your yard or something. When that didn't work, I called the church office, and it was closed, and I was starting to get desperate. With nothing but time on my hands and no other options until Monday morning, I googled you."

"You ran up and down every street in Southport and googled me?" Abel's tone carried a certain amount of disbelief.

"I know. I know," Cullen said. "When I say it out loud, I sound like a real stalker. Don't I?" Cullen held up his hand. "But I promise I'm not."

Abel raised an eyebrow and folded his arms across his chest. "Go on."

Damn if he's not enjoying this just a little bit. Or maybe a lot. Cullen rolled his eyes. "Anyway, I found an article about you online, announcing your appointment to the Southport Baptist Church. It said you would reside in a church-owned residence on Caswell Street. So I walked up and down Caswell Street until I finally saw Dottie outside and struck up a conversation. And before you say anything, yes. I added the reverend title to my name. I thought it would lend credibility."

"Apparently it worked."

Cullen smiled, feeling a little proud of himself. "Yes. She told me you lived right next door. For all the good it did me. You were gone by then. That reminds me. You never said where you actually went."

Cullen waited for some sort of response, but what came was most certainly not what he was expecting.

Abel smiled broadly and launched himself into Cullen's arms. "I can't believe you did all that to find me. Cullen, no one has ever cared enough about me to do anything like that."

Cullen, for what seemed like the hundredth time since he'd met Abel, swallowed the lump in his throat. Here he was thinking Abel was going to be upset with him because of the measures he'd taken to find him, and instead Abel was flattered. The man never ceased to amaze him.

"Are we gonna run or not?" Cullen asked, trying to lighten the weight of the moment.

Abel kissed his cheek and started up the stairs. "Give me five, and I'll be right down. Make yourself at home."

Cullen peeked through an open door off of the foyer into a powder room. He walked through the living room into a dining room and eventually the kitchen and keeping room. The place was nicely furnished. Very neat and clean. But it was… what? What was the word he was looking for? Cold? Unwelcoming? Yeah, both of those words certainly applied.

It was also something else. It was sterile. Looking around Cullen saw not one personal thing of Abel's. Not one iota of his personality. No pictures of himself. Of course Cullen didn't expect to see any family pictures because Abel had no family, but besides that, the place just didn't feel like a home. It didn't feel like a place Abel would live or even be comfortable in. Suddenly Cullen was very grateful for all the pictures he and Cole had taken over the years. They served as his memories now, which was all he had left.

Stop it, Cullen. This is about Abel. Not you.

Luckily before Cullen could send out invitations to his own pity party, he heard Abel's footsteps on the stairs. He started back for the foyer and met Abel on the last step.

"How do you like my palace?"

"It's very nice."

"Nice? Yes. But I've never felt at home here. It has never felt like my place."

"Maybe 'cause it's not," Cullen said. "This place is not you, Abel."

"You're right. And whatever it is to me, it's not even gonna be that for much longer."

"That's right," Cullen said. "The church owns it, so if you resign, you'll need to vacate the property. Any idea where you'll go?"

Abel hesitated. "Not really. I haven't thought that far ahead. Baby steps. Remember? For both of us."

"Baby steps," Cullen repeated.

"You take the lead," Abel said.

Cullen pulled out his phone, started his running application, and put his earbuds in his ears. "You okay with five miles?"

"I'm not a runner, but I'll give it my best." Abel put earbuds in as well.

"Okay, let's go."

Both men waved to Dottie, who was still rocking steadily on her porch, as they ran down the steps. They turned left on Caswell Street and headed to the Riverwalk, intercepting Cullen's normal route. Before long they both seemed to be lost in their own heads.

CHAPTER ELEVEN

CULLEN'S STEPS were steady and his breathing was regular, but his brain was on maximum overload. He looked to his right. Abel seemed to be keeping up with him just fine. Abel. What was he going to do about Abel? Cullen hadn't meant to tell him about his dreams, but the words had flowed out so effortlessly, he hadn't been able to stop himself. In the end he was glad he'd done it. Abel's take on Cullen's dreams was a little different but essentially as valid as Cullen's. Yes, it could have been some higher power bringing two lost souls together. And Cole may have even had a hand in it. But the more likely scenario to Cullen was that it was his own guilty conscience trying to in some way validate his leaving Cole behind and moving on with his life.

Whatever the truth was, it didn't really matter. If Cullen was even going to think about living again, he would have to do a great deal of soul searching. And what about Abel? If he took Abel down this path along with him and it didn't work out, what would happen to Abel? Abel had been let down by too many people already, and Cullen wasn't about to add his name to the list.

"Time: nine minutes forty-two seconds. Distance: one mile. Current pace: nine minutes thirty-eight seconds. Average pace: nine minutes forty-two seconds. Split pace: nine minutes forty-two seconds."

Cullen waited for the British woman to stop talking and pulled out one of his earbuds. He looked at Abel. Abel had taken off his shirt and tucked it in the back of his shorts. When had that happened? His torso was glistening with sweat, and Cullen watched Abel's pectoral muscles tense and release with each pump of his arms. His hair was falling over his forehead, and his eyes were alert. And damn if he wasn't matching Cullen step for step. To top it all off, Abel was singing. Cullen listened to the lyrics as Abel sang. "My Soul's Been Satisfied." He must be listening to gospel music.

Cullen tried to remember a popular gospel singer's name. He smacked Abel on the arm. "Hey, Michael W. Smith. We're doing good. Under ten minute miles. You okay?"

"I'm good," Abel said. "I'm really enjoying this. Who is Michael W. Smith?"

"Never mind." Cullen put his earbud back in his ear, realizing his little joke had backfired. He chuckled to himself. *I've run to a lot of different music, but never gospel.*

Cullen peeled off his T-shirt and tucked it away as well. The warm sun felt good on his skin, and he was at the point where the run kicked into autopilot. It wasn't long before Cullen was thinking about Abel again, though. He cursed himself because it seemed that Abel dominated his thoughts these days. That realization surprised him.

Rationally, the only thing that stood between him and Abel getting to know each other better was Cole and his memory. So he decided to take Cole out of the equation for just a few minutes. He told himself he wasn't forgetting him. He was just trying to figure all this out logically, not emotionally. If Cole were never in the picture, would Abel be someone Cullen would pursue romantically? The answer came much quicker than Cullen would have imagined. *Hell yeah!*

Abel was gorgeous. Built like a brick shithouse. Sexy as hell. Funny. Smart. And he had a certain something that Cullen had only seen in one other person. And… times up. Cole was back in the equation. But at least Cullen had his answer.

But what if Cullen got involved with Abel and then decided he couldn't go through with it? He couldn't do that to Abel. It was obvious Abel was already attached to him, and Cullen knew why, but that attachment could also be an unhealthy one. Even if their friendship went no further than what they'd already done, Abel was going to be affected when Cullen did decide to leave. Whether it was tomorrow or in the spring when he had to go back to P-town. It was as though Cullen was in a no-win situation.

"Time: 12:22 p.m. Distance: 2.5 miles."

Cullen once again pulled one of his earbuds out. He smacked Abel, who was still singing, on the arm again. "Time to turn around."

Abel nodded. "I can't believe we're already halfway through."

He's only three years younger than I am. But he looks like he has enough energy to run all the way to Wilmington.

Two and a half miles later, they reached the Riverwalk again, and the run was over. Cullen was no closer to deciding what to do about Abel, but for some odd reason, he felt better. He stopped at one of the swings, put his T-shirt back on, and sat. Abel put his own T-shirt back on as well and sat beside him, and the two men didn't attempt to speak until they each caught their breath.

"Looking good, Pastor Weston," a passerby said. "You okay?"

"I am, thanks," Abel replied breathlessly. "Just a long run."

The passerby nodded, smiled, and kept going.

"You're quite the celebrity," Cullen said when he had enough air in his lungs to form a complete sentence. "Does everyone in this town know you?"

"Pretty much," Abel said. "The different congregations of the local churches often socialize together, and our church even throws a yearly picnic for all the other denominations in town to come together in the spirit of all loving one God despite the differences in beliefs. Trust me. Everyone knows your business."

"So how are you gonna be yourself in Southport with so many prying eyes? I would think it'd almost be like living in a fishbowl."

Abel waited a long moment to respond. "I thought about this a lot on our run. The short answer is, I don't think I will be able to."

Cullen was totally caught off guard by that admission and now very curious. "What's the long answer?"

Abel sighed. "I guess I stay closeted for a little while longer. At least until I can decide what to do. I don't want to be homeless, and right now I have no place else to go. I have some money saved, but it won't last forever."

"You'd really leave Southport?"

"Yeah. I mean… I don't think I can stay. Besides, without the church, there's really nothing to keep me here."

That statement rang through Cullen's head. *There's really nothing to keep me here.* While he mulled it over, he turned his attention to the river, locked onto a passing boat, and stayed with it until it rounded the bend and was no longer visible.

Cullen had known all along he would eventually leave Abel. Leave Southport. That was inevitable. Either to move farther south or to head back up north in the spring. He had to. His shop and what little life he had was in P-town. But what he hadn't considered was Abel leaving him. That stung for some stupid reason. But why? He'd known Abel for less than a week. Had Abel so quickly become some sort of lifeline for him? If not, then why would it matter who left whom? Cullen had sensed the moment he'd met Abel that the man had needed him. Needed a friend. That's why he'd stopped. But could he actually need Abel just as much?

"And then there's the job situation." The sound of Abel's voice brought him back to the conversation. "The church and being a pastor is the only thing I know."

"Just because you leave your current church, doesn't mean you can't minister. You can join another denomination," Cullen said. "One that's more open and accepting."

"Like the Episcopal Church?"

"Sure! Why not? But if you don't want to minister, you can always teach. Abel, you're an educated man. You can do anything you want. It just depends on your calling." Cullen turned to Abel and resisted the urge to take his hand. "Look! Instead of thinking about this as an ending, try to think about it as a beginning."

Cullen experienced a flash of déjà vu ministering to Abel this way. The surprising thing was it didn't feel as foreign as he thought it would. In fact, it felt almost natural. Almost normal.

"Where will you go?" he heard himself ask as if on autopilot.

Abel squinted against the afternoon sun and gazed out over the water. "Good question."

Abel can join you on T-Time! Cullen heard the words in his head, but he wasn't about to acknowledge them. *Where did that come from?*

Instead he asked, "Is there someplace you've always wanted to visit or live?"

"Hadn't thought much about it. I've always been in the South. It's where I feel the most comfortable."

Cullen inwardly flinched. Again for some odd reason, Abel's words pricked him somewhere deep down. Did he want Abel to say New England? That was silly. Why would he? Pushing the thought aside, Cullen asked, "What about Atlanta, Miami, or even Charleston? They have big gay communities in all three of those cities. And then there's the West Coast. Or New England."

Abel seemed to be pondering his response. "I have no idea. But I'll definitely have to give that some serious thought. What's New England like?"

"Beautiful in the summer and extremely cold in the winter. It has a quintessential small-town feel. Every place except Boston. That feels as big as Atlanta or Miami, but the Cape and the Islands are very cool."

Abel nodded. "Sounds nice."

He was quiet for a long while, and Cullen was starting to get concerned.

"Enough!" Abel said at last, getting to his feet. "It's a beautiful day, and I don't want to waste it talking about my screwed up life."

Cullen stood. "Okay. What would you like to do?"

Abel didn't hesitate. In fact, Cullen would bet his life Abel already knew where he was headed with this conversation. "I followed your exercise regimen. How about you follow mine?"

"The gym?"

"If you think you can keep up, old man."

Cullen saw the playfulness in Abel's green eyes, and it warmed him. It was good to see him being so lighthearted and fun, especially knowing the life decisions he would be making very soon. "Who are you calling an old man?" Cullen asked. "Bring it on."

Abel punched Cullen in the upper arm and took off running. "Last one to my house buys lunch." He looked back over his shoulder and smiled.

"Oh, no you don't." Cullen took off after him.

Cullen was sleek. He had a runner's body and passed Abel almost halfway there. Abel was fast, but he was built like Popeye, massive upper body and arms that made him almost sluggish. Abel was built for strength, and Cullen was built for speed.

Leaning on the fence, his arms folded over his chest and feet crossed at the ankles, Cullen held up a finger when Abel finally got there. "I think we're going to the Frying Pan for lunch."

"Fine," Abel said, bent over, hands resting on his knees. "My car keys are inside. Man, you're lightning fast."

Cullen followed Abel through the gate and playfully jabbed his fingers in Abel's sides as they walked up the steps. "And calling me an old man just made me drive harder. So thanks for the motivation." Cullen started laughing when Abel squirmed and started hopping around like a jester.

"Stop it. I'm ticklish," Abel whined. "My keys are in the pocket of your sweats in my bedroom. You wanna see upstairs?"

"Sure." Cullen climbed the stairs behind Abel and started jabbing his fingers in Abel's back and tickling his waist. Abel began to squeal and dance his way up the stairs, which just urged Cullen on more. When they reached the top of the stairs, Abel ran toward his bedroom, but Cullen was right on his heels.

He tackled Abel in the doorway, pushing him into the room, and they both ended up in the middle of Abel's king-size bed with Abel on his back and Cullen straddling him. Cullen began to tickle Abel's muscular body enthusiastically, and Abel started pleading and begging him to stop, laughing hysterically.

In one quick move that surprised the heck out of Cullen, Abel sat up, stole a quick kiss, and pushed Cullen to his side, the force sending Cullen's legs and arms flailing and reaching for anything to grab on to. Abel's fists closed around Cullen's wrists and pinned them to his sides, where Abel's knees held them firmly in place. Abel flashed a sinister grin and rubbed his hands together as if to say *payback is a bitch.*

It was Cullen's turn to plead and beg as Abel was merciless with his efforts. Abel started by squeezing his fingers into Cullen's armpits and wiggling around and then running them down to Cullen's waist and repeating the process. By now Cullen was laughing so hard he was afraid he might pee himself. *Would serve Abel right if I peed in his bed.*

Cullen cackled and howled between pleading and cursing until he was flailing on the bed like a fish out of water. Abel outweighed him by at least twenty-five pounds, and there was no way he was going to overpower him. He'd just have to wait until Abel decided to show him some mercy.

"I—I give." Cullen was laughing so hard he had a tough time getting the words out. He had no idea when he'd last laughed so hard and so long.

"What's that you say? You give?" Abel's voice was full of naughtiness.

"Yes! Yes! I give!" Cullen said.

Abel stopped his incursion, and their laughter started to settle into chuckles until their eyes met and all forms of hilarity halted.

Cullen stared up at Abel, focusing on the little droplets of sweat glistening on his upper lip. When Abel used his tongue to lick the droplets away, Cullen felt a definite tug in his groin. Abel released Cullen's hands from his sides and brought them up, stretching them over Cullen's head and pinning them there. His cock jumped again when Abel shifted and leaned forward. Cullen closed his eyes when Abel's lips touched his. They were warm and wet and tasted of perspiration, and the combination was sending pulses right to Cullen's groin. Cullen's cock was stiffening between them.

Abel pressed his tongue against Cullen's lips and sought entry. Cullen welcomed the intrusion and made a weak consenting sound that surprised even him. The sound seemed to give Abel more confidence, and he took the kiss deeper. The combination of the kiss, Abel's weight straddling him, and his movements had Cullen hard as a rock. He was nearing the point of no return when he realized this was make-or-break time. The discord of doubt plaguing Cullen for days was suddenly silenced by an urgent craving that could not be denied.

It wasn't fair to Abel, and he needed to stop now if he wasn't prepared to go through with this. There was no doubt going to be fallout. But how much and how bad? Could his and Abel's friendship survive?

Without breaking the kiss, Abel released Cullen's hands, stretched out, and settled at Cullen's side. Abel was trembling ever so slightly as he moved his hips forward and pressed his erection against Cullen's thigh.

Alarms were sounding in Cullen's head. *Stop now or there's no turning back.*

But Cullen didn't stop. The warmth of Abel's body was beginning to spread through him, and he realized he needed Abel. Wanted him.

Yes. There would be hell to pay, but he'd deal with that later. Right now he was numb to everything but Abel's touch. Feeling

Abel so close to him, wanting him, so willing, was all he could think about. Cullen rolled over, stretched his long body on top of Abel's, and ground their erections together. This time it was Abel who released a whimper of approval, which in turn just about sent Cullen spiraling out of control. It had been a long time for him, and if he was going to last for any reasonable amount of time, he needed to take control.

Breaking their kiss, Cullen sat up and again straddled Abel's thighs. Cullen pulled his T-shirt over his head and tossed it to the floor. He then offered his hands to Abel and pulled Abel up to a sitting position. He grabbed the hem of Abel's T-shirt and pulled it up over his head. An encouraging smile graced Abel's lips, and again Cullen was warmed to his core.

Cullen leaned forward and covered Abel's lips in a crushing kiss, and Abel immediately opened to him. In the midst of their tongues thrashing and exploring, Cullen had a sudden need to protect and take care of Abel. He wanted to make up for all the love and encouragement Abel had missed out on as a child.

"Abel. Be sure, okay? There's no turning back from this."

"I've never been more sure of anything in my life," Abel said breathlessly.

"Whatever *this* is," Cullen whispered, "we are in it together. You're not alone. Okay?"

Abel nodded.

Cullen began to explore Abel's body, running his hands up and down Abel's chest. He studied every muscle, counted every freckle, committed everything to memory.

Cullen again bent down and kissed Abel, dragging his tongue across Abel's bottom lip and biting gently. Even through their shorts, Cullen felt Abel's cock, bound tightly between them, stiffen with desire.

Abel was rubbing his hands up and down Cullen's back, his nails scratching lightly and tantalizing Cullen's bare, goose-bump-covered skin. Cullen withdrew and trailed moist and satiny kisses down Abel's throat, chest, and abdomen. Then he licked his way back up Abel's torso, and Abel arched his back and hissed when Cullen stopped at his nipple, bit lightly, and then licked one and then the other. Cullen slid down to the foot of the bed, removed his shoes and socks, and stepped out of his running shorts.

Abel's eyes were wide and full of wonder as Cullen stripped down to his underwear and climbed back up the bed, gripping the waistband of Abel's shorts and slowly pulling them down and off.

Cullen climbed back up and straddled Abel again. Giving Abel a look up and down, he offered him one last out. "Are you sure you want to do this?"

"God, yes," Abel said without hesitation.

Cullen chuckled inwardly at his choice of words.

"But more importantly, do you?" Abel asked.

Cullen considered Abel's question. In a matter of days, Abel had woven himself into the fabric of Cullen's being. Their lives had gotten so tightly wrapped up in each other's that Cullen was almost fearful about where this might lead. But right now, in this very moment, he wanted Abel.

"Yes," Cullen said. "Right now I need you desperately."

"What about tomorrow?" Abel asked.

"At this very minute, I couldn't care less about tomorrow."

"Cullen?" Abel said with worry in his voice.

Cullen stopped him before Abel could say another word. "Please stop worrying about me and enjoy this. I want to make your first time as special as I can."

"But?"

"No buts."

Cullen slid his body all the way down to Abel's erect cock. It was straining for release, and Cullen could tell Abel wouldn't last very long. He gripped Abel for the first time, feeling the weight of his cock, the silky warm skin, the bulbous head.

Abel dropped his head and hissed as Cullen ran his hand up and down Abel's hardness.

Cullen slid down farther, and Abel cried out when Cullen placed his wet mouth over Abel's erection, still sheathed in his cotton boxer briefs, and ran his teeth along Abel's length. Cullen stopped at the head of Abel's engorged cock and surrounded it with his moist lips. Cullen noted that he and Abel were about the same length, but Abel had more girth.

Cullen looked up at Abel, who was watching him intently, gaze riveted on every motion of Cullen's mouth running up and down his cock. "Feels so good," Abel said when their eyes met.

Cullen slid his finger under the waistband of Abel's underwear and pulled them down to Abel's knees. Abel's cock plopped out and landed on his stomach, pointing north. Abel gasped and fisted the sheets when Cullen swallowed him and buried his face in his groin. His musky scent was strong and mixed with sweat, and the aroma had Cullen's cock twitching in his underwear. He came back up and went slowly down again, Abel thrusting his hips up to meet every advance.

Releasing Abel's cock, Cullen slid down to Abel's balls and took them into his mouth one at a time. Cullen tugged and sucked on them gently until Abel was gyrating under him and moaning incoherently. Cullen pushed farther down, and Abel opened his legs wider, giving him all the access he needed. Running his tongue as far down as he could go in this position, Cullen licked at the sensitive stretch of skin between Abel's ball sac and his opening. Abel moaned louder. Cullen lifted Abel's legs and buried his face in Abel's ass. He gently ran his tongue over Abel's opening, and Abel literally came up off of the bed, arched his back, and dropped back down again. Taking that as a sign, Cullen drove his tongue as deep as he could into Abel's tight opening, retreated, and dove in again—licking, circling, probing. Abel was once more gyrating, humming incoherent sounds.

Lowering Abel's legs, Cullen again took him in his mouth. Abel tasted of his salty prerelease, and Cullen licked and teased the head of Abel's cock until Abel gripped his hair. "Please, stop."

Cullen froze and looked up at Abel. *Damn! I knew this was too soon.*

Abel must have seen the panic written all over Cullen's face. "No, Cullen. It's not that. It's so good, I'm about to come. I want to taste you. I want to experience it all."

Cullen expelled a sigh of relief as Abel reached down, hooked his hands under Cullen's arms, and pulled him up to him. "Kiss me, please."

Cullen obliged as their cocks rubbed up and down, coming dangerously close to spewing his load all over Abel's stomach. Way too soon.

Luckily Abel had other ideas. Abel kicked the rest of the way out of his underwear, and Cullen saw them fly across the room as Abel rolled him over onto his back. But instead of gently kissing his way down Cullen's torso like Cullen had done to him, Abel went straight for Cullen's underwear, pulling them off and diving face first into Cullen's crotch. *So much for foreplay.*

But what Abel lacked in subtlety, he more than made up for with his ability to work Cullen's length. Abel apparently had no gag reflex, and he took Cullen all the way to the back of his throat, held him there as long as he could hold his breath, and then slid back up and used his tongue to circle Cullen's sensitive head.

"Are you sure this is the first time you've done this?" Cullen gasped.

Abel let Cullen slip from his mouth and peered up at him. He smiled. "I promise. I may or may not have seen a porn video or two in some weak moments, but that's the extent of my training."

"Boy! You sure are a quick study—and an eager beaver."

"Thank you. I've waited a long time for this. Now are you gonna do a running commentary, or are you gonna lie back, enjoy, and allow me to explore and experience?"

"Sorry." Cullen rested his head back, closed his eyes, and enjoyed the attention Abel was bestowing on him. It had been so long since he'd felt the warmth of another, had the desire to be close to anyone, and he kept waiting for the guilt to come, but so far it hadn't.

Cullen gasped when he felt Abel's tongue run around his sac and under his balls, dip a little lower, and then come back up again. Apparently following Cullen's lead, Abel lifted Cullen's legs over his head, and Cullen grabbed them and held them in place. Abel spread Cullen's cheeks and ran his tongue quickly over Cullen's opening. He did it again, and this time it lingered. He circled, licked, probed, and then licked again. He sucked on Cullen's balls, jostled them around in his mouth, tugged on them, and then let them slide out. Abel lowered Cullen's legs and again went down on Cullen.

Cullen was getting close, and he wanted to come with Abel, so he shifted around, and Abel released him. "Can I show you something?"

"Sure."

"It's called sixty-nine." Cullen slid down the bed a little. "Now turn around so your feet are at the head of the bed and give me access to you."

Abel moved, adjusted, and readjusted until his length was aligned perfectly with Cullen's face. In return Cullen was right where he needed to be. Both men took the other in, and within seconds they were in a rhythm that was blowing Cullen's mind. Abel was a natural, and at this rate, Cullen wasn't going to last very long.

Cullen must have been doing okay because Abel said something that sounded like, "I'm gonna come," and then moaned loudly, and his entire body stiffened. Feeling Abel's warm blasts shooting down his throat pushed Cullen over the edge as well. He felt himself release, spurt after spurt, and to Abel's credit, he didn't gag or choke but swallowed every drop and milked Cullen's cock until there was nothing left but a very sensitive head.

After bleeding Abel dry as well, Cullen pulled Abel up to him and kissed him deeply, trying to convey all the passion he was feeling for the first time in so long. For Abel.

When they came up for air, Abel said. "I can taste myself on your tongue. That is so hot."

Cullen chuckled.

"Thank you," Abel went on. "My first time was everything I hoped it would be. That is, once I allowed myself to think there might be a first time."

Abel laid his head on Cullen's chest and began tracing that line of hair like he'd done the night before, but this time he was able to follow it all the way down to Cullen's groin and back up again. Cullen didn't understand the fascination, but he relaxed and enjoyed the sensation.

They lay in silence for the longest time, Cullen listening to Abel's breathing and bracing himself for the guilt that was surely to follow. But so far it hadn't come. He'd had sex with Abel, and the earth hadn't opened up and swallowed him whole. *Abel may have, but the earth hasn't.* And he wasn't an emotional wreck.

Yes, he was experiencing emotions. But none that made him want to jump up, grab his clothes, and bolt down the stairs naked. He was content lying here with Abel in his arms, and that alarmed him a little.

When the guilt finally worked its way into Cullen's head, he was prepared for it. The problem was he'd prepared for the wrong kind of guilt. He wasn't feeling guilty because he'd had sex with Abel. He was feeling guilty because he *didn't* feel guilty. *Cullen! You're a severely screwed-up lad.*

As Cullen's mind processed his emotions one by one, he realized it wasn't moving on without Cole that had wrecked and exhausted him so badly, it was the battle he'd waged against doing just that. He'd fought so long and so hard to hold on, it had become his private war. He'd come to Southport to try and rejuvenate his memories of Cole. That much he'd admitted. But what he hadn't asked himself was, why should he have to? *Could it be you've already subconsciously let go of Cole? That it was happening little by little with each passing day, and somehow you knew it? And that's what terrified you so much?*

The more Cullen contemplated this new possibility, the truer and more real it felt deep in his soul. He'd not been able to consciously grieve for Cole. That was a fact. But was it possible his subconscious had taken over and started the grieving process for him? Had Cole been slipping away from him all along, but he hadn't allowed himself to feel it happening?

Jesus, Cullen! How could you be so dense when it comes to your own life? You've been trained for this.

Cullen thought about his dreams. He would have loved to believe that they had everything to do with Cole and God bringing him and Abel together. And at one time he would have been open enough to allow that thought to resonate. Only now the more likely scenario was that the dreams had everything to do with him trying to justify and process what had already subconsciously happened. In Cullen's mind, he heard the clicking of the locks as the shackles at his wrists and ankles released. He felt light enough to rise off of the bed and float away.

He sighed heavily. *I think I'm gonna be all right.*

"You okay?" Abel asked, interrupting his thoughts.

"Surprisingly I am. I'm still processing it all, but yeah, I think I'm okay. You?"

"I'm better than okay. There's just...." Abel's voice trailed off.

"There's just what?"

"Next time—and I'm not assuming that there's gonna be a next time—but if I'm lucky enough to have a next time with you, I want to do more."

"More?" Cullen asked, pretty sure he knew what Abel meant. But he was going to make the newbie work for it.

"You know… more."

"No. I don't know."

"Anal," Abel whispered like it was a bad word or something.

"Oh, anal! *That* more," Cullen said out loud.

Abel slapped him on the chest. "Now you're just teasing me."

"I am," Cullen admitted. "And it's kinda fun."

Which promptly earned him another slap.

"Okay. Okay. Anal it is. Next time."

"Yes!" Abel pumped his fist in the air. "So there *is* going to be a next time."

"Who am I to deny you some good anal loving if you want it so badly?"

"Thanks. I think."

"You're welcome. You know my mother always said it was the quiet ones who were the kinkiest."

Cullen looked down at Abel's face, and it was blood red, but he hadn't denied it.

"I guess we're not going to make it to the gym. Are we?"

"You complaining?" Abel asked, a lighthearted tone in his voice.

"No complaints from me. Not right now anyway."

"I'm not going to ask you to talk to me about what you're feeling, but if you want to, I'm here."

"Thanks," Cullen said. Meaning it. "When I know what I'm feeling, you'll be the first to know."

"That's all I can ask for," Abel said, squeezing Cullen's torso.

"Do you have a bathing suit?" Cullen asked.

"Yeah. Why?"

"What do you say we pick up lunch and go to the boat and get some sun? We won't have many days like this before winter sets in."

"Sure."

CHAPTER TWELVE

ABEL CRUMPLED the wrapper from his chicken sandwich into a ball, stuck it under his sun pad, and downed the last of his soda. "That hit the spot. Man, I was starved."

Cullen laughed. "I think you were starved for more than just lunch."

"I do believe you are right, sir. And luckily both of my appetites have been sated. For now, anyway."

Abel leaned over and rested his elbow on Cullen's sun pad. "Who knew one could work up such an appetite just by having sex."

Cullen raised his hand. "I did."

They had picked up sandwiches from the Yacht Basin Provision Company, went straight to the boat, put on their suits, slathered on sunscreen, and took their lunch out onto the bow.

Abel slid his shades down over his eyes, leaned back, and linked his hands behind his head. It was about three thirty, and the sun was still bright and warm and felt great. Abel felt great. Alive for the first time in his life. And he had Cullen to thank for that. He could only liken the experience to being starved for thirty years and then being offered a smorgasbord of one's favorite foods.

Cullen had been sweet, attentive, and most of all, patient with him, taking the time to show him things he'd never experienced. But that hadn't surprised him at all. What had surprised him most about the entire experience was how naturally it had come to him and how natural it all felt.

He hadn't lied when he'd told Cullen he'd only seen a couple of porn videos. The rest he'd done purely on instinct, and it had been the best experience of his life. But what had stayed with him the longest was Cullen's unique scent. Burying his face in Cullen's crotch had introduced him to a distinctive musky and extremely manly scent that had been pure heaven flowing through his nostrils and had driven him wild with desire at the same time.

Oh my God. And the sweetness of Cullen's butt. He couldn't believe he was thinking about this, but Cullen's butt was the hottest damn thing he'd ever seen. With the exception of Cullen's beautiful penis. *You can say dick in your head, Abel. You're not in the pulpit.* Yeah. Beautiful dick.

No, Abel. Don't get distracted. Back to Cullen's butt. He'd heard people use the term "smelling like ass" to describe a nasty smell, but apparently those people hadn't smelled Cullen's ass. It was clean and tasted absolutely sweet. He then wondered if his tasted as sweet.

And his orgasm. Jesus! He'd felt it building from deep within his gut, and when it descended upon him, he couldn't hold back his moans of pleasure as multitudes of colors exploded behind his eyes. And then there was the cuddling afterward. Being in Cullen's arms after they'd shared such an emotional and physical experience had been the most comfortable he'd felt in his life.

He remembered listening to Cullen's heart beating, a little fast at first and then settling into a steady and calming rhythm that had almost lulled Abel into slumber. But then he'd heard Cullen sigh, and the sound had concerned him. He'd known Cullen would probably regret what they'd done, and he'd tried as best he could to prepare himself for the rejection, but so far it hadn't come. Cullen seemed okay. Maybe he'd had some sort of emotional breakthrough when it came to Cole. But only time would tell.

Abel had secretly thought about New England when Cullen had mentioned it as a possible place to live. He wondered what it would be like to live there with Cullen. That was stupid, right? They'd just met. But maybe if Cullen spent the winter here with him and something worked out between them, it could happen.

But for that to work, Abel would have to keep his job and live in the closet for another six months. Could he do that? In actuality if he wanted to be with Cullen, he really had no choice. If he quit the church now, he would be forced to move away, and since it was way too soon to even think about anything lasting with Cullen, he would probably never see him again. But something or someone had brought Cullen into his life for a reason, and he didn't think he could give him up that easily. *Time, Abel. Give this some time. You've lived in the closet all these years; six more months won't kill you.*

Besides, you'll still have Cullen, albeit behind closed doors. But at least he'll be in your life.

"You're awfully quiet over there."

"Just basking in the afterglow," Abel teased.

Cullen leaned up on one elbow. "I don't know if it's me or the sun, but you are sort of glowing."

"Oh no, Cul. The sun can take no credit for any of this."

Cullen's expression suddenly changed, and Abel couldn't quite get a read on it.

"I'm sorry. Did I say something wrong?"

"No," Cullen said through a sigh. "It's just... well. Cul is what Cole used to sometimes call me. Hearing it after so long took me by surprise. That's all."

Damn! Everything was going so well, and I have to go and blow it. "I'm so sorry," Abel said. "It just came out. I won't make that mistake again, I promise."

Cullen reached over and laid a hand on Abel's forearm. "It's okay. You didn't know. And truth be told, in a weird sort of way, it sounded good to my ears."

Abel breathed a sigh of relief. He laid his hand on top of Cullen's. "I really am sorry."

Cullen looked out over the waterway. "Forget it. I shouldn't have said anything. Like I said, it just took me by surprise. That's all."

"No. I'm glad you told me. I want to know these things. I want... to know Cole and hear about the life you shared with him, but only when you're ready. I mean... it's obvious to me how much you loved him, and for you to love him so much, he must have been an extraordinary man."

"He was," Cullen whispered. "Look! The sky is so beautiful. And the sun is about to drop below the horizon."

Abel didn't know whether Cullen was really watching the sunset or simply changing the subject, but either way he would let him take the lead. Cullen would tell him about Cole in his own time, and Abel was prepared to wait.

Cullen had been right about the sky. The sun was hovering just above the horizon to the west. Abel watched it drop lower and lower until it was completely gone, leaving a wispy sky swirled with various shades of magenta, orange, and pink mixed together, all reflecting off of the billowy clouds, creating an array of fluffy, colorful figures. "The perfect ending to the best day of my life," Abel mumbled almost to himself.

"And just think, it's not even over yet," Cullen said with a smile and a wink.

"I stand corrected. But really. For the very first time in my life, I feel alive and full of hope for the future. And I owe that all to you."

"I don't know about that," Cullen said, getting to his feet. "But I am so happy for you. You've waited far longer than most to be happy, and no one deserves it more than you."

"Thank you." Abel got to his feet as well.

"Why don't we get cleaned up and start thinking about someplace for dinner."

"Can I pick the place?"

"Sure. What did you have in mind?"

"A quaint little place called Live Oak Café up on North Howe. It's one of my favorites."

Cullen nodded. "I'd love to give it a try."

SEVERAL HOURS later they were back at the marina and walking down the dock, their appetites now sated, simply enjoying comfortable conversation and each other's company.

The restaurant had been a great choice, and Cullen now knew why Abel liked it so much. It was an old house, and the multiple dining rooms were all small and only held a couple of tables each, so it was very private. He wondered if that was the reason Abel had selected it, but if so, he understood. If they were seen out too many times together, the local tongues might start to wag, and that could be bad for Abel.

Abel proved to be an exceptional conversationalist. He was smart, had a great sense of humor, and was an overall pleasure to be around. They'd talked about Southport, P-town, boats, T-shirts, the church, and everything else under the sun. The conversation had flowed easily, and Cullen had thoroughly enjoyed himself.

Since his recent revelations regarding Cole, Cullen seemed to be handling things a lot better. It wasn't like he still didn't miss Cole. That would never change. But now the pain and longing seemed a little more manageable. The important thing was, he now understood what had been driving him, and now he could deal with it better. Also realizing he'd been letting Cole go gradually had made all the difference and had seemed to take the present fear and desperation away. But the real question was, would this truce he'd called with his emotions hold?

"Look!" Abel pointed down the dock. "There's a new boat." He smacked Cullen on the arm. "I'll race you to the dock house." Abel took off running.

"Oh, no, you don't," Cullen said, taking off right after him.

Cullen might be a seasoned long-distance runner, but he was nothing if not a sprinter. He caught up to Abel in seconds, passed him up, and was waiting for Abel when he reached the dock house. "Damn! Not again."

"Yep. Again."

"Just wait until I get you to the gym," Abel said, looking up from under his eyelashes. His lips were now a little pouty, and it was absolutely adorable on him. Cullen looked at Abel, and a smile twisted his lips. He ran the backs of his fingers along Abel's jaw and then took him into his arms and whispered into his ear, "I'm sure you're gonna kill me at the gym."

Abel stilled for a second and then melted into Cullen's embrace, and it was the most glorious feeling to have him fit so perfectly. For just one second, he allowed himself to think about love at first sight. He hadn't believed in that crap until he'd met Cole. Could it happen to him again? Could he be so lucky? He remembered how he'd been so drawn to Abel when he'd first seen him sitting on that park bench. The connection he'd felt. *Does lightning strike in the same place twice?*

"WHATAYA SAY we call it a night?" Abel looked around to make sure they were alone, took Cullen by the hand, and led him toward the boat.

When they were safely inside, away from the prying eyes of Southport, Abel stepped up to Cullen, placed his hands on Cullen's chest, and kissed him gently. He slowly and deliberately released the buttons of Cullen's shirt, one at a time, and pulled the shirttails out of Cullen's jeans. Abel ran his hands over Cullen's bare chest, down his sides, up his back, and once again to his chest. He brushed his thumbs over Cullen's nipples, pinched them gently, and released.

Cullen sighed and threw his head back. Abel studied him closely, and when Cullen dropped his head to face him again, Abel held eye contact with him for one eternal moment. Cullen finally cupped Abel's face and kissed him so completely, Abel felt it down to his toes. Cullen gripped the bottom of Abel's golf shirt, and Abel lifted his arms. The shirt glided over his head and flew across the saloon. Cullen stared down at Abel with such an expression of desire that it took his breath away. He'd never been desired. Never been looked at that way. Something shone in Cullen's eyes that Abel wanted to call love, but he didn't dare. Instead he fought back the tears welling up in his eyes and put the thought out of his head.

Cullen's callused hands roamed freely over Abel's broad muscular chest, caressing him in a way that made Abel's entire body tingle. Abel closed his eyes and licked his lips in anticipation as Cullen again cupped his face and brought their lips together in a slow kiss that churned emotions deep inside, emotions Abel never knew he had. Cullen took Abel's hand and led him down to his cabin, but once there, Abel took control, covering Cullen's mouth with a wet, desperate kiss as he moved him toward the bed. When the backs of Cullen's legs hit the mattress, Abel pushed with all his might, and Cullen went down on his back, looking up at him in surprise. Abel flashed his best seductive smile—not that he'd ever practiced a seductive smile before—and hoped it conveyed his longing for Cullen, his desire to have him.

Cullen was breathing heavily and sweat was starting to glisten on his skin as Abel stared down at him. *He's so beautiful.* Now that he knew he could be Cullen's undoing, Abel wanted nothing more. He suddenly realized he'd succeeded in reaching an unreachable man, gotten inside a heart that had been locked away for almost two years. *I can't take this lightly. I have a responsibility to protect the heart I've penetrated no matter what it takes.*

Abel dropped down to Cullen's feet and slipped off Cullen's loafers and socks without ever breaking eye contact. He came up on his knees and released Cullen's belt and jeans and pulled them down and off, along with Cullen's underwear. Cullen's long, lean, naked, and extremely chiseled body was a sight to behold. In the dimly lit cabin, the little bit of silver hair at Cullen's temples glimmered brightly against his otherwise black mane, and his eyes were a brilliant blue. How could Abel be so lucky? How could this have happened to him?

Wasting no time, Abel unbuckled his belt, toed out of his shoes, and removed his jeans and underwear. Lastly, he peeled off his socks and then looked down at Cullen, whose eyes were hooded with lust. The sight made Abel groan and bite his bottom lip. Abel climbed onto the bed, and when his skin touched Cullen's, his nerve endings suddenly caught fire, as if a thousand volts of electricity went flowing through him at breakneck speed. Chill bumps instantly covered his body, and the hair stood up on the back of his neck.

"Come here." Cullen pulled Abel up to him, wrapped him in a strong embrace, and kissed the top of Abel's head. "You are one gorgeous man. You know that?"

Abel didn't concur, but he felt the blush creeping up his face and fought the urge to disagree. "Thanks," he whispered instead. In reality, whatever Abel was, it was because of Cullen and the confidence he'd given Abel to live his true life.

Abel raised his head and looked up at Cullen. He ran his palm along Cullen's jaw and hoped his eyes conveyed all the emotions jumbled inside him. Abel opened his mouth to speak, but Cullen pressed his index finger against Abel's lips.

"Shh.... It's okay. I know."

Cullen rolled over, pinned Abel beneath him, and buried his face in Abel's neck. He nibbled on the sensitive area where Abel's neck met his shoulder and then trailed soft kisses down Abel's torso and back up again. Wedged between their bodies, Abel's cock was painfully hard, and it jumped each time Cullen moved or shifted, sending waves of pleasure coursing through him. When Cullen slid down again and took Abel into his mouth, the warm, wet sensation caused Abel to tremble with anticipation.

"Cullen!" he gasped, arching his back and fisting the sheets, desperately needing something to hold on to.

Abel shuddered when Cullen circled the delicate skin under the head of his cock and then swallowed him, holding him there until he could no longer breathe before sliding back up. Cullen gripped Abel and began moving his hand in unison with his mouth, up and down, applying a slight suction one stroke at a time that was about to undo Abel completely. Abel released his grip on the sheets and ran his hands through Cullen's thick black hair, riding Cullen's head up and down as he passionately tortured Abel with pleasures beyond his imagination.

"Stop," Abel moaned, and Cullen withdrew. "I'm getting too close, and I want this to last. I want *more*."

Since they'd already established what *more* meant, Abel and Cullen both knew what Abel was anticipating, and the thought made Abel shiver with expectation. He trusted Cullen and had no doubts of any consequence. Still, fear of the unknown was electrifying and frightening at the same time.

Abel wanted to feel Cullen moving inside him, needed to be one with him, but why the urgency? Something was nagging at Abel just beyond his comprehension, and it lingered there like a dark cloud hanging overhead.

Cullen was now kissing his way up Abel's stomach and chest, and after teasing Abel's nipples, he smiled and hovered just above Abel until their eyes met. "Are you sure?"

Abel hesitated for a split second and then nodded. "I need this."

"I need this too," Cullen said. "For so many reasons."

Cullen reached over to the bedside table, retrieved a bottle of lubricant, and as if something had just dawned on him, cursed under his breath. "I forgot about condoms. Haven't used them in ten years."

"Are you... okay?" Abel asked sheepishly.

"Yes. I'm HIV negative if that's what you're asking. And so was Cole. We were a monogamous couple, and I haven't been with anyone since his death. I would never put you or anyone else at risk. But if you'd rather not, I totally understand."

"No," Abel said. "I trust you."

Cullen raised an eyebrow. "Remind me later to chastise you for being so trusting."

Abel rolled his eyes. "And remind me later to ask you not to talk so much during sex."

"Duly noted."

Cullen hastily kissed Abel on the lips and then settled between his open legs. Abel was still rock hard, his length lying flat against his stomach. Cullen flipped open the top of the lube bottle, gripped him, and drizzled the lube over his hand as he stroked Abel's length. The combination of the lube and Cullen's slick, callused hand moving up and down him teased another shudder out of Abel. Cullen raised Abel's legs over his head, and as Cullen had done earlier, Abel grabbed his ankles and held his legs in place. The position was not altogether uncomfortable, but he felt exposed and vulnerable. He kept reminding himself this was Cullen, and he trusted him.

With one hand still on Abel's cock, Cullen spread Abel's ass cheeks with the other hand and ran his tongue over Abel's virgin opening. Abel sucked in a breath and released it. The sensation was all too brief, and Abel wanted to feel it again.

As if reading his mind, Cullen licked him once more, this time lingering and wiggling his tongue for a few moments. Every muscle in Abel's body contracted and then relaxed again when Cullen withdrew.

The tingling sensations in his groin and ass were driving Abel wild with passion, and he secretly wished Cullen would do it again. Deeper. Longer. But he was too shy or embarrassed to beg.

Finally, Abel's wish came true. Cullen's warm, wet tongue started licking and prodding continuously. Wiggling and probing. And as if that alone wasn't pleasurable enough, Cullen started moving his hand up and down Abel's length in time with his lashing tongue. Abel instinctively started to wiggle and thrust his hips up into Cullen's hand, riding the waves of pleasure that surged through him. Abel could feel his opening relaxing with each movement of Cullen's tongue. And then the laving ceased.

Abel sighed and silently cursed Cullen for stopping until he heard the flip of the lube bottle's top again. Soon after, he felt Cullen applying the slick liquid to his opening, swirling his finger around the sensitive nerve endings, probing ever so gently, and then swirling again.

Every muscle in Abel's body tensed with delight and anticipation, but he didn't have to wait very long. Cullen slowly slipped one finger inside him, and Abel nearly came off of the bed, his internal voltage meter hitting the red zone. But when Cullen passed over a particular spot inside Abel's body, Abel screamed as a jolt of something coursed through him. Passion. Electricity. Boundless desire.

Cullen withdrew, and Abel gasped loudly in protest. But when Cullen pushed in again and began to move in and out, Abel felt a stimulating rush of pressure each time Cullen brushed his prostate. Without conscious intent Abel let out a moan that seemed to go on forever.

"You okay?"

Abel heard Cullen's voice somewhere in the distance, but for some reason his tongue and lips just wouldn't come together to form a response.

"Abel? Do you want me to stop?"

Sounding closer now, Abel heard the concern in Cullen's voice and somehow forced his tongue to cooperate with his brain. "No, I'm good. Better than… actually… great." He knew his words were fractured, but it was the best he could do.

Abel flinched and tensed for a second when he felt a slight pinching sensation as Cullen stretched him open, obviously slipping a second finger inside him. The sensation was odd and a little uncomfortable, but not at all bad. He relaxed and his body adjusted rather quickly to the intrusion.

Cullen worked his fingers in and out of Abel in a slow, steady rhythm that sent surges of pleasure up and down Abel's spine. The more Cullen moved his fingers, the more relaxed Abel became, his body naturally compensating. Abel was a mindless mass of male flesh, and he was enjoying every minute of it.

"You ready?" Cullen asked.

Abel nodded but didn't speak. He heard the familiar sound of the flip top and opened his eyes to see Cullen coating his own length in long, slow strokes. That sight was almost enough to send him over the edge before they even got started, so he closed his eyes again tightly and tried not to imagine what Cullen was doing.

The next time Abel opened his eyes, Cullen was positioning himself, and Abel felt the head of Cullen's length pressing against him, skin smooth against Abel's slicked opening. Abel tightened his grip on his ankles and did his best to relax.

You want this, Abel. Relax!

Cullen pushed slowly, purposefully, inside Abel's body, and Abel cried out as though Cullen had pierced his heart. The pain. The pinching. The stretching. All seemed unbearable for a short second, but Cullen never took his eyes off Abel, and it was what Abel needed. To see his face. To hold their connection.

Then Cullen stopped and gave Abel time to adjust, and Abel felt himself slowly relaxing around Cullen's girth. Cullen supported Abel's legs now, and Abel let go of his ankles, bringing one hand instinctively to his erection and the other to Cullen's thigh.

Abel stroked himself, an act that began to turn the discomfort into something else. Not pleasure yet, but not quite pain either. When Cullen started to move again, Abel was ready. Cullen slowly pushed in farther and farther until Abel felt the slight tickling of Cullen's crotch hair against his balls.

The pain was definitely subsiding and being replaced with a feeling of fullness. Odd and unfamiliar, but not altogether unpleasant. Cullen retreated, pulling out slowly, and when he slid against Abel's prostate again, Abel cried out, "God in heaven." When Cullen pushed in again, what was left of the pain turned to instant pleasure. Every nerve ending in Abel's body was on fire. His pulse was racing and his heart was pumping at breakneck speed. Every time Cullen pulled out and drove back into him, Abel felt sweetly and thoroughly penetrated. His moans were now flowing freely, and the sounds emanating from his own body seemed foreign and completely out of his control.

It was almost as though Cullen had turned Abel's skin inside out and was lightly teasing every one of his nerve endings simultaneously. Abel felt his orgasm forming from deep within. His balls tightened, and he stroked himself in time with Cullen's thrusts.

"Cullen! I'm so close."

"It's okay, Abel. I'm right behind you."

Abel locked eyes with Cullen as the man steadily pounded into him. He continued to stroke his length, bringing on the spasms that would lead to his gut-wrenching release.

Surfing on the first wave of his orgasm, Abel cried out as pearls of white liquid covered his neck and chest. Abel pumped harder as his body convulsed, the remaining waves dotting his torso from his pectorals down to his belly button. He milked himself until he was completely empty.

"Abel!" Cullen moaned as he pumped frantically.

Abel watched Cullen through a haze of ecstasy as his lover convulsed and muttered incoherently until his thrusts finally slowed and he sighed in the aftermath of his orgasm and collapsed on top of Abel.

They lay there breathless, wrapped in each other's arms. Abel was pulsating with a feeling so new he couldn't really understand it. He realized he was no longer the man he had been a few days ago, or even a few hours ago. He felt so alive and so filled with a warm light he imagined he must be glowing.

And then in a split second, doubt worked its way into Abel's brain. He quickly identified the familiar feeling teetering just beyond his grasp. *Fear.* In an instant he questioned whether Cullen could ever really be his. Cullen seemed to belong wholeheartedly to Cole. Abel had known this after that first dinner when Cullen had broken down and told him about Cole.

If God had truly sent Cullen to him, why would he take him away again? At that moment Abel understood a little about what Cullen had been going through losing Cole.

Abel had no doubt in his mind now that Cullen would eventually leave him. His life and his business were in New England, and Cullen had given no indication he would ask Abel to join him. That was a reality Abel would have to get used to. He knew he wasn't strong enough to leave Cullen, so he had no other choice but to enjoy the ride until it ended.

Just keep your feelings in check. That's all you can do.

He tightened his grip on Cullen as tears threatened to spill from his tortured eyes.

"Was that okay?" Cullen's voice penetrated his thoughts.

"Amaz—" Abel's voice cracked. He swallowed hard. "That was amazing."

"You were amazing," Cullen said. "The way you moaned when I moved inside of you. You were driving me mad with desire."

Cullen climbed out of bed and came back with a warm wet towel. Abel allowed Cullen to clean him from his chin down to his nether regions and then watched as Cullen tossed the towel back into the head.

Abel rolled onto his side, and Cullen pulled him back against his chest, trailing little kisses across Abel's back and shoulders. "Thank you."

Abel sighed. "Because of you I'm a different man. I will never forget you, Cullen."

Cullen wrapped his arm around Abel's waist and pulled him even closer. Abel dissolved into him, wanting to stay there forever.

I love you, Cullen Kiley.

CULLEN LAY awake long after Abel had drifted off to sleep. His arms were still securely wrapped around Abel, and Abel was breathing calmly and rhythmically.

There were so many emotions coursing through Cullen. He thought about Cole. He knew Cole would want him to be happy. He would have wanted the same for Cole if their positions had been reversed. Except Cole wouldn't have been so stupid and pigheaded about it.

And then there was Abel. Cullen was surprisingly okay with what he and Abel had done earlier. No flashbacks of Cole had entered his head. He hadn't screamed Cole's name when his release seemed imminent. What did that say?

His eyes had locked on to Abel's, and they hadn't wandered. He was right there with Abel. Feeling his emotions, sensing his wants and needs. They had been perfectly in tune with each other. How could all of this happen in less than a week? And something Abel had said right before he drifted off to sleep rang through Cullen's head. "Because of you I'm a different man. I will never forget you, Cullen."

What did Abel mean by that?

CHAPTER THIRTEEN

A COUPLE of weeks had gone by, and Cullen and Abel had settled into something almost resembling a relationship. Every hour that Abel wasn't working, they spent together. Abel had seemed distant at times, something Cullen couldn't quite put his finger on, but the distance seemed to disappear just as quickly as it came. Maybe Abel was just getting used to his new life and Cullen.

It was Sunday morning, and Cullen was sitting alone on the flybridge finishing his third cup of coffee. Abel had left just under an hour ago, claiming he needed to put the finishing touches on his sermon. He was in the pulpit this morning as Pastor Williams was away on church business. Abel had asked him to attend the service, and not wanting to disappoint Abel, he'd reluctantly agreed. But Cullen had to admit he was as jittery as a long-tailed cat in a room full of rocking chairs.

This was the first time he would be in church for an actual service since Cole's memorial mass. Yeah, he'd stopped in at Abel's church as a last resort when he was so worried about him, and the experience had been a bittersweet one, but that was just him and his thoughts. Now he would have to listen to God's word, and he wasn't sure he was ready for that. Abel had asked very little of him during their time together, and so he'd promised.

Just before the service started, Cullen slipped into the church and took a seat in the last row on the end—close to a door in case he needed to escape. He looked around nervously and locked eyes with Abel, who was sitting off to the side of the pulpit with his Bible in his hand. Abel flashed a crooked smile, obviously very aware of why Cullen had chosen that particular seat, and Cullen smirked and then smiled broadly.

Cullen felt himself relax a little when the music started. Music always had that effect on him, but this music wasn't at all like his church—his former church—where the organ blared as the procession made its way down the aisle. This was less pageantry and had more of a celebratory feel to it. When the song ended, Abel took the pulpit and welcomed everyone, regulars and visitors alike, glancing at Cullen a time or two. When he got into his sermon, Cullen was not surprised to see that Abel was a natural in the pulpit. He was sincere, which was the most important thing, but he was also commanding and soft-spoken at the right times. His sermon today focused on the death of Jesus. He talked about how much of an injustice it had been, but that according to the Bible, it also happened according to the plan and purpose of God. Abel examined the Crucifixion in light of the doctrine of providence from the perspective of God, Jesus, and the human participants. He preached that although the Crucifixion was a mystery we cannot fully understand, the injustice of the Crucifixion accomplished God's plan from eternity to demonstrate the breadth of his love by redeeming sinners.

Cullen thoroughly enjoyed the sermon, but he couldn't help but think Abel had preached it partly on his behalf because of the way he felt about God taking Cole from him. And if the truth be told, his defenses were starting to crumble, little by little. Sitting in this strange church, listening to another man preach, Cullen realized how much he missed the fellowship of the church. Everyone here was different in some way, but they were all there for one reason: to worship. And that made their differences fade away, at least for one hour on a Sunday morning. Cullen also sensed that he missed his relationship with God, but that was a little harder to admit to himself right now.

After the service, while Cullen was waiting for Abel on the steps of the church, Agnes Williams approached him.

Abel had warned him that she'd been her normal busybody self, quizzing him about his and Cullen's friendship, how they knew each other, and specifically about Cullen and his church, so Cullen had been on guard.

"Good morning, *Reverend*," she'd said in a haughty tone. "How nice to see you supporting your seminary mate Pastor Weston."

"Oh, we were never seminary mates. And good morning to you as well, *Mrs*. Williams."

"But you said—"

"What I said was a mutual friend from the seminary told me Abel was assigned here, so I looked him up when I was passing through."

"Oh, silly me," she said. "I must have misunderstood. You've been in Southport… what? A couple of weeks now? I imagine you're probably thinking of moving on soon."

"Not really. I like Southport, and I'm on no schedule, so I have all the time in the world."

"Tell me, Reverend, how *does* an Episcopal priest get so much time off?"

"I'm on leave at the moment," Cullen said without missing a beat. "I live in a seasonal town with very few parishioners in the winter months, so the church assigns an interim priest so I can have the winter off."

"How nice. At any rate, I'm a little surprised to see you here."

"Oh? Why is that?"

Agnes chuckled. "Come on, Reverend, it's no secret the Southern Baptists think very differently from the Episcopalians."

"That's very true." Cullen dipped his head and picked at something on the steps with the toe of his shoe. When he looked back up, Agnes was glaring at him.

"But we all have one thing in common. Don't we?" he said.

"I suppose that's true. But—"

"You ready?" Abel yelled, cutting Agnes off and bouncing down the church steps.

"I am," Cullen said. "Good to see you again, *Mrs.* Williams."

"Same here, *Reverend.*"

WHEN THE two men reached the sidewalk and crossed the street, Abel stopped and looked back. Agnes was still standing on the steps watching them, one arm crossed over her large bosoms, a finger on her chin, and her head cocked to one side. She waved, and he waved back before he turned and they started walking.

"I swear that woman is two Corinthians short of a Bible and the nosiest thing I've ever seen," Abel said, picking up his pace. "Was she pumping you for information?"

"Yeah."

Cullen related their conversation to Abel.

"Something about her rubs me the wrong way," Cullen said. "I can't quite put my finger on it, but I'd watch out for her if I were you."

"I will. Hey, how did you like my sermon?"

"It was great. You're a natural in the pulpit."

"Really? I'm always a little unsure of myself and my sermons. They seem old and boring." Abel paused. "I would love to make them more relevant to today. You know? Something young people can identify with, or something that brings the message in a way that makes more sense today."

"Why don't you?"

"Pastor Williams," Abel said flatly. "He believes in teaching the Word in its truest form. As it was written. Just old school, I guess. And since he's the boss, I have to follow his rules."

"But I don't understand how anyone can believe something written over two thousand years ago is still relevant in its purest form. Yes, the meaning and the message will always be relevant. But today's society needs more. Can't he see that faith is getting harder and harder to sell? We are no longer a society that follows blindly. The Word and the message need to make sense to people before they will embrace it. It needs to be explained so that it can be applied to life today."

Abel stopped, put his hands on his hips, and smiled broadly. "Now this is the passion I knew was boiling just below the surface of Reverend Cullen Kiley."

Cullen blushed. "Sorry. I guess I got a little carried away."

"Don't apologize. I love to see you this way. The church needs more passion like this."

"I don't know about that, but thanks. It felt kinda good to rant just a little."

"Cullen! You are wasting your calling. I'm gonna get you back in church if it kills me."

"That will probably kill us both." Cullen chuckled nervously and stuck his hands in his pockets. Obviously wanting to change the subject, Cullen looked up at Abel through his lashes. "You hungry?"

Abel smiled. *Well, lookee there! I do believe Cullen is working me.* Abel knew, and apparently so did Cullen, that he had an insatiable appetite for food. He was always hungry and usually ate up to six meals a day. The funny thing was, that constant hunger had carried over to the bedroom, which had totally surprised him. He'd never been one to masturbate often. What little pleasure it brought him was usually over in seconds, and most times it was more for release than a source of pleasure.

But in the past two weeks, he and Cullen had made some form of love every night and sometimes even twice a day. And based on Abel's newly awakened libido, he didn't see that slowing anytime soon. Luckily Cullen seemed to be right there with him.

In the past two weeks, though, he'd had bad days and good days. He still couldn't shake the feeling that he and Cullen were on borrowed time. Sometimes he was able to push it to the back of his mind and focus on the here and now, but other times, especially after sex when they were quietly holding each other, the fears would come rushing back at him full force. He could tell Cullen had sensed his mood swings, but he hadn't pressed Abel on it.

Unfortunately, the weight he'd been carrying was getting heavier with each passing day, and instead of diminishing, the feeling was becoming increasingly real. He was now more convinced than ever that Cullen was going to leave him, pure and simple. He was sure of it. But what could he do about it? In actuality there was little he *could* do. He'd been struggling to keep the proverbial feelings of abandonment at bay, but a lifetime of people leaving him was a very hard thing to forget, much less overcome. Abel had been trying as best he could to prepare for it, but no matter how much he prepared, he knew it was going to hurt like hell.

"I'll take that as a yes," Cullen said, smiling back and gesturing over his shoulder. "Since we're already here, what about brunch at Ports of Call?"

"Okay by me."

While they waited for a table, Abel nodded to several groups of people from the church, who were already seated, and a few more familiar faces who came in behind them. Everyone said hello and complimented Abel on his sermon. Abel introduced Cullen to them all as his good friend Cullen Kiley, who was visiting from New England. *Reverend* Kiley was no longer on the table.

Brunch was great, albeit interrupted several times by church members stopping by to say hello and how much they'd enjoyed Abel's sermon this morning.

They were stepping onto the main dock at the marina when Abel's phone rang. He fished it out of his coat pocket, looked at the caller ID, and quickly put the phone to his ear. "Pastor Williams?"

"Abel, I'm sorry to bother you, but do you think you could meet me in my office. Say, in fifteen minutes."

"I… I guess so. But I thought you were out of town?"

"Just got back about thirty minutes ago. And again, I'm sorry to inconvenience you, but it's important."

"Okay. Sure," Abel said, hearing concern in Pastor Williams's voice. "I'll be there shortly."

"Thanks, Abel."

Abel ended the call.

"That was Pastor Williams," he said.

"I gathered as much." Cullen cocked his head to one side. "Is everything all right?"

Abel shrugged. "I don't know. But he wants to meet in his office in fifteen."

"Did he say why?"

"No. And he didn't sound quite like himself either," Abel admitted. "I hope everything's okay."

Cullen squeezed Abel on the shoulder. "You'll never know unless you head over there. I'll be here when you're through."

"Okay. I'll see you in a bit."

ABEL HURRIED back to the church. He had a weird feeling about this. He'd never before been summoned after service or after he'd left for the day, which left him very uneasy.

When Abel reached the church office, Agnes was at her desk, which was very unusual for a Sunday afternoon.

"He's waiting for you." Agnes didn't even bother to meet his eyes.

Abel opened the door to the pastor's office and froze. He felt like he was interrupting a meeting already in progress. Pastor Williams, along with four other neighboring pastors he recognized and one tall willowy man he did not, were all seated in a semicircle with one empty seat, which Abel assumed was his.

"Close the door behind you and take a seat, son," Pastor Williams said, nodding to the empty chair.

Their expressions were laced with concern. Or was that anger? Or even worse, disappointment? Abel knew this wasn't going to be good. But what had he done? Had this morning's sermon been so bad that Pastor Williams needed backup to help chastise him? If so, who was the other man?

Pastor Williams interrupted his thoughts. "Before we get started, Abel, please turn off your cell phone and put it in this box." The pastor held a cardboard box of cell phones in front of him. "We really don't want to be interrupted."

This must really be bad. "Okay." Abel powered off his phone and dropped it into the box with the others. "Do you mind if I ask what this is all about, Pastor?" he said, looking around at the others.

"Unfortunately, Abel, it has come to our attention that you've been engaging in some very unhealthy behavior for an associate pastor of a Southern Baptist Church. Behavior, according to our beliefs, not even suitable for a layperson."

Abel shook his head as if he wasn't hearing correctly. "Excuse me?"

Pastor Williams cleared his throat. "Abel. After witnessing some rather strange behavior, Agnes did a little research regarding your friend, the Reverend Cullen Kiley from Provincetown. And what we uncovered is very disturbing to us."

Abel's stomach turned. He instantly knew where this was going, and he surely wasn't prepared for it. *Calm down and take a deep breath. You need to play this cool.*

"Okay," he answered, aware that the nervousness was clear in his voice. "What might that be? And furthermore, what does it have to do with me?"

"For starters, he is no longer a reverend of the Episcopal Church, but continues to use the title when it suits him."

"He *is* an ordained priest who is on sabbatical."

Pastor Williams didn't respond and continued. "Secondly, he is a homosexual who *was* a priest in a predominantly homosexual community, and as you know, we strongly denounce homosexuality."

"*Is* a priest," Abel corrected, looking around the room. "And I ask again." The nervousness in his voice gave way to a certain level of annoyance. *The nerve of them!* "What does the fact that Reverend Kiley is a gay Episcopal priest have to do with me?"

"You've been seen on a regular basis hanging out at the Riverwalk with *Mr*. Kiley."

"Reverend Kiley," Abel corrected again.

Pastor Williams waved his hand. "Not to mention jogging through town half naked. At the local gym. At several local restaurants. And on his boat in what we consider very intimate settings." The pastor hesitated. "Consuming alcohol, Abel! And you've spent the night on his boat every night since he arrived."

"That's not true," Abel said. "But I want to get this right. In your opinions—" He made eye contact with each of the other attendees. "—it's unacceptable behavior to spend time with a friend, exercise, and eat dinner. Is that what you're saying?"

"Abel!" Pastor Williams slapped his hand on his knee. "You know it's more than that, and so do we. This is an intervention, and you have some very serious decisions to make."

Abel stood so abruptly it sent his chair toppling over. "An intervention?"

"Calm down, Abel," one of the other pastors said. "Getting angry with us is not going to help anyone, least of all you. We're here to help you, son."

"It sounds more to me like you're here to condemn me. Judge, jury, and executioner all wrapped up in one." He looked around the room again. "Or should I say, *five?*"

"That's just not true. Are you telling us our presumptions are wrong?"

Abel righted his chair.

It's now or never, Abel. You needed time to convince Cullen to take a chance on you, but you no longer have that time, which leaves you two choices. Deny, send Cullen away, and go back into the closet, ignoring the fact that you feel alive for the first time in your life.

Or tell the truth now, lose your job, and maybe Cullen. It's far too soon for Cullen to even think about another relationship, and after this scandal breaks, you'll need to leave town for sure. Your best chance is to admit it now, take your licks, and hopefully Cullen won't abandon you. But if he does, at least you know who you are now.

Abel absentmindedly rubbed his shoe over a stain on the carpet right between his feet. He finally looked up. "You're not wrong."

"We didn't think so. Abel, please allow us to save you."

Chapter Fourteen

Cullen was pacing now. He'd tried sitting quietly. Watching television. Listening to music. But nothing had taken his mind off of the fact that he'd been tracking the time closely since three o'clock, and there was still no sign of Abel. He was worried sick. It was not like Abel to not touch base with him, and when he'd attempted several times to reach Abel, the call had gone straight to voice mail. He was putting on his shoes, about to go over to the church, when he heard a knocking on the hull of the boat. He looked at the clock again. *Six o'clock. Thank God. But why is Abel knocking?*

He hurried up the companionway stairs and crossed the cockpit, and his heart dropped when he saw Agnes standing on the dock. "Mrs. Williams? What are you doing here? Is something wrong with Abel?"

"May I speak with you Rev—I mean, *Mr.* Kiley?"

Mr. Kiley? This can't be good.

"Sure." Cullen gestured for Agnes to come aboard.

She climbed the steps and joined Cullen in the cockpit. "Please have a seat," he said. "I'll ask you again. Is something wrong with Abel?"

"Abel is not hurt if that's what you're asking."

Cullen felt a flood of relief wash through him. "Then where is he?"

"He's with my husband, four other regional pastors, and a counselor."

"In heaven's name, why?" Cullen asked.

"Mr. Kiley. Please allow me to be blunt and get right to the point." Agnes's voice was laced with darkness.

Cullen nodded tightly.

"I'm here, Mr. Kiley, to ask you to leave Southport immediately."

Cullen couldn't believe what he was hearing. "Leave Southport? Why?"

"For Abel's sake."

"What do you mean *for Abel's sake*?" Cullen asked, his voice a combination of frustration and anger.

"My husband and I, as well as most of the congregation, know what has been going on between the two of you."

"What?"

"Oh, don't act so surprised. We're not dumb country hicks who can't see our hand in front of our face. And you Episcopalians claim to be God-fearing people."

"First of all, *Agnes*. Episcopalians are not God-fearing people. We are God-loving people. There is a difference. Secondly, what I do is none of *your* business."

"But what Abel does with you *is* my business. And the church's business and the congregation's business. My God, you didn't even try to be discreet."

"*What* are you talking about?"

Agnes dug her phone out of her purse, tapped the screen a couple of times, and handed it to Cullen. "Pictures speak louder than words."

Cullen took the phone from her and looked at the screen. A picture of him and Abel at the Riverwalk, his hand on Abel's thigh, stared back up at him.

Before he could explain, Agnes chimed in. "Keep going," she said. "There's more."

Cullen slid his finger across the screen and another picture came into view. This time it was him in Abel's arms in this very boat the night he broke down telling Abel about Cole. He flipped through a dozen more photos of him and Abel in various locations around town—sometimes touching, sometimes not. Having dinner. Running through town. Shirtless on a swing at the Riverwalk. At the gym. Abel sipping what Cullen knew was a shot of bourbon. The two of them sunning on the bow of the boat.

"You've been stalking us?"

"Not me," Agnes said innocently. "And I don't think I would go so far as to call it stalking."

"What in the hell would you call it, then?" he asked angrily.

"I like to call it concerned members of the congregation standing up for their beliefs."

"That's a load of crap, Agnes. And you know it. You people are nothing but a bunch of bigoted sinners masquerading as Christians."

"That's very strong language coming from a homosexual former Episcopal priest who's more than likely gonna burn in hell for his lifestyle."

Cullen was flabbergasted. *These people have been investigating me.*

"Don't look so shocked. I can google. Just fifteen minutes on my computer yielded a plethora of information."

"No wonder you're God-fearing," Cullen sneered. "You spend your life sitting in judgment of others, in his name. But you also know that one day you'll be held accountable for that behavior when your own judgment day rolls around. Funny how that works, isn't it?"

Agnes flinched, and Cullen knew he'd thrown her off kilter. He'd dealt with her kind before. She was all fire and brimstone, but he knew her type well, and he knew the Bible even better. He could take her on quote for quote if it came to that, and come out ahead every day of the week. But while she was wavering, he took the opportunity to twist the knife just a little more.

"And furthermore, Agnes. Do you think God approves of you manipulating his Word into something you can use to discriminate against and hate other people who don't share your beliefs? Do you really think He's gonna pat you on the back for that kind of bigotry? I think not."

Agnes huffed, grabbed at a stray piece of hair, and stuck it behind her ear. She straightened and seemed to regain a little of her composure. "When the time comes, Mr. Kiley, I will answer to my maker, just as you will. And if he sees fit to condemn me, I'll see *you* in hell."

"I hate to burst your bubble, but I won't be in hell."

"That's not for you to decide, Mr. Kiley."

"You're right. But I know my God, and He loves and respects me just as I am. The way *He* made me. And as much as it hurts me to say, He even respects you, as difficult as that may seem. Unlike you, *Agnes*, He forgives sins, even yours, because that's who He is and what He does. But you will have to ask for that forgiveness. And I can only hope I'm there to see you beg for it."

"You can hurl insults at me and my faith all night long if you like, but that's not going to help Abel. The only thing that will help Abel is for you to leave Southport now."

"Like hell," Cullen said through clenched teeth. "Now get off my boat so I can go to that church of yours and save the man I love from the likes of you people."

Agnes's eyes widened with apparent shock, and Cullen smiled, surprising even himself with that admission. *The man I love!* He'd known his true feelings were simmering just below his consciousness, and the natural instinct to protect Abel was exactly what he needed to bring them to the surface. God and Cole had sent Abel to him. He was sure of that now. And Abel needed him now more than ever. He wasn't going to let Abel down.

"I'm afraid that's not possible," Agnes said.

"And why not?"

"Because he's not at the church."

"Then where is he?"

"He's in the middle of an intervention."

"An intervention?" Cullen repeated.

"It might be too late for you, Mr. Kiley, but it's not too late for Abel. We're gonna save that boy from the likes of you and at the same time from burning in hell."

Cullen's anger was building by the second, and he needed to find Abel. "You better tell me where the hell he is, or I'm calling the police."

"You can call whomever you like. We're not holding Abel against his will. Who do you think asked me to come here?" Agnes asked.

When one is strong, the other is weak. The power always shifts between foes, and the time has come. Now it was her turn to twist the proverbial knife. Cullen felt weak in the knees. He grabbed the handrail and steadied himself, unable to process what Agnes had just said. "Abel sent you here to ask me to leave?"

"Not so righteous now, are we, Mr. Kiley?" Agnes looked away, apparently not wanting to meet Cullen's eyes.

"But why?" Cullen sat on the steps to the flybridge and buried his face in his hands.

"Because he's agreed to go into an extensive therapy program and knows he has no chance of succeeding if you are still here."

"What kind of therapy program?"

"It's called conversion or reparative therapy."

Cullen had studied that as part of this ministry. "Are you kidding me? Oh my God, Agnes. Every medical, scientific, and government organization in the United States and Britain have expressed concern over this therapy and how potentially harmful it is. And you're gonna subject Abel to this? Why didn't you just try and pray him straight like the rest of the Bible beaters?"

Agnes straightened her posture. "It has been proven to work, Mr. Kiley. And don't you worry. We'll be doing a lot of praying as well."

For the first time, Cullen realized that Agnes really did believe she and the other members of the God squad, in their own way, were trying to help Abel.

"Mr. Kiley," Agnes said, softening her voice. "If Abel wants this, don't you think he at least deserves the chance to try? Deserves a chance to be normal?"

"Normal? By whose standards, Agnes?"

Agnes clapped her hands together. "God's standards! He wants this! The least you can do is support him."

Cullen stood. "I want to see him. I need to hear this from him."

"That's not possible," Agnes said. "My husband is driving him to a facility upstate as we speak."

"Upstate where?"

"I don't know."

"Shit," Cullen cursed. "This can't be. Abel would never agree to something like this. What did you hold over his head or use against him? What did you threaten him with?"

"Come on, Mr. Kiley. We're not evil people. We're only trying to help someone who doesn't want to be a homosexual. We would do the same for you if you asked us to."

"Don't hold your breath for that, Agnes."

"I figured as much," Agnes sneered.

"How long will he be gone?" Cullen asked feeling more and more defeated by the minute.

"I don't know the answer to that question, but I was told it could be months. These things take time." Agnes stood. "Mr. Kiley, do yourself and Abel a favor and just let him go."

"I don't know if I can do that."

"You have no choice," Agnes said. "If you believe everything you've told me about your God, then you have to believe if you and Abel are meant to be together, God will bring him back to you."

"Sometimes even God has trouble asserting his will when there are underhanded outside forces at play." Cullen met Agnes's gaze. "And I don't for one second doubt that you, your husband, and his band of merry pastors have used underhanded tactics to influence Abel in his decision."

"I'm sorry you feel that way." Agnes stood. "Whether you believe it or not, we are doing this for Abel. Good-bye, Mr. Kiley."

"Bullshit!" Cullen said.

Agnes narrowed her eyes and pursed her lips together like she was insulted. She started down the aft steps. When Agnes stepped on the dock, she stopped and looked over her shoulder. "Such language for a supposed priest."

Cullen's blood was boiling now. "I guess you just bring out the best in me, Agnes. And I'm sure I'm not the first person, clergy or nonclergy, you've made angry enough to use foul language. That," he added, "I'm sure comes naturally to you."

"Well," Agnes huffed. She raised her chin and stomped down the dock back toward the shore.

Cullen sat down and cradled his head in his hands again. He was in a state of disbelief. *Did that just happen?* Feelings of helplessness, fear, uncertainty, doubt, and disappointment all began to spread through him, each fighting for front and center. He'd only felt that way one other time in his life, and he refused to go there. Not yet anyway. He couldn't. If he did, he might never recover!

CHAPTER FIFTEEN

ABEL WAS mentally and physically exhausted. It was four o'clock in the morning, and he'd been essentially locked in a room all night long. His captors had been relentless.

The inquisition had started off with the counselor, who had questioned him for hours about his homosexual tendencies. When he'd first experienced them, if and when he acted on them, how far he'd gone, and if he could change, would he want to be a heterosexual.

That was the funny part, because if this had happened a month ago, Abel would have jumped at the chance. But Cullen had changed all of that for him. *Cullen*! He wanted so badly to call Cullen. To let him know he was all right. He needed him now more than ever, but he'd put his phone in that damn box.

After Abel had told the counselor he had no desire to be heterosexual, the willowy man had finally given in and left the room. Next the pastors came in as a group and prayed over him. They exhorted the Father, the Son, and the Holy Spirit to remove the evil homosexual desires that plagued him. Then they sent in the counselor again, and the questioning started all over.

Each time this happened, Abel assured the counselor he still did not want to change and just wanted this to be over. They all tried to convince Abel he was no longer in control of his actions and all this was the work of the devil. When he still refused, they threatened him with eternal damnation if he didn't accept the help they were offering him. Next they came in one at a time, each using different tactics to try to convince him to go to treatment.

When they'd finally exhausted every method they had and nothing seemed to work, they started in on Cullen—how evil he was and how he'd recruited and corrupted poor Abel. They even threatened to contact the Episcopal Church and have him excommunicated for his actions and… for impersonating a priest! Abel had to laugh at that one. Now they were just desperate and reaching for anything.

If Abel had really wanted out, he could have easily busted down a door or broken out of a window, but he allowed this lockdown to go on for one reason and one reason only. To prove to these men, beyond a doubt, that he was in control of his actions, in love with Cullen, and wanted no part of what they were offering him. And if he had to give up one night of his life to do it, so be it. Besides, he hadn't once felt like he was in any danger. He knew these people, except for the counselor, and they were basically good people, albeit steeped in their beliefs.

In the end they had pleaded with him, threatened him, threatened Cullen, promised him salvation—like that was in any of their control—and gone so far as promising to get him his own church. They even told him that when he succeeded, he would become a role model for other struggling homosexuals.

By the time the last pastor had slammed his Bible shut in exhaustion, it was seven o'clock in the morning. He'd resigned his position to Pastor Williams, turned over his keys to the church, and agreed to be out of the church residence by noon. Abel had no idea where he was going, but he didn't care. All he wanted right now was to get to Cullen and enjoy him for however long they had left.

Abel stepped out of the church and stopped on the front steps. He looked up at the sun and closed his eyes. The rays were warm on his face, and he felt like the weight of the world had been lifted from his shoulders. He ran from the church to the marina without stopping once. He was operating on adrenaline and desire and a renewed energy for his future with Cullen. He turned into the marina, ran down the dock, and stopped short.

T-Time's slip was empty.

CHAPTER SIXTEEN

CULLEN HAD still been awake when the sun peeked above the horizon. He'd spent the entire night on the flybridge, unable to bring himself to lie in the empty bed he and Abel has shared every night for the last two weeks. He wouldn't have been able to sleep anyway. He needed to think. To decide what to do. Abel *had* prayed endlessly to be straight, and if he was getting this opportunity, would he take it? These people could be very persuasive, and if Abel dropped his guard for one second, they would have him eating out of their hands. Not because Abel was weak, but because they knew exactly what they were doing. Especially if they brought a counselor into the mix.

But still. Abel hadn't called him or answered his calls. Did that mean something? And Agnes had said that Abel was the one who'd asked her to come to the boat and ask him to leave.

If Abel really wanted this opportunity, how could Cullen stand in his way? *If he really wants it.*

But much to his surprise, in a roundabout sort of way, Agnes had had the biggest impact on him. Did Cullen believe the propaganda he'd been spewing to her about his God? He had, wholeheartedly, at one time, but things had changed. As of late, they had started to change again, and he owed that all to Abel.

Had God brought Abel into his life simply to help him move on and finally bring him back to the church? Maybe Abel was never meant to stay with him. But how could his God, the God he was telling Agnes about, do that to him twice? Give him someone to love and then take him away so easily?

In the end he decided to leave. But it was going to be hard to leave Abel and Southport behind, for so many reasons. Cullen's and Cole's memories here came into play too, but this was mostly about Abel. In less than a month, Abel had buried himself so deeply in Cullen's heart that it was hard to think about not seeing his smiling face every day. How had he become so attached to the man in such a short time?

But for some strange reason, Cullen was very calm. Deep down he didn't think his and Abel's time together was over. It might be over for now, but not forever. If he was going to embrace his faith again, he needed to do it unconditionally, and it was now or never. *Have faith, Cullen. Just have faith!*

The adrenaline that had flowed freely through Abel's veins just seconds ago was now nothing more than a slow drip. Staring at that empty boat slip, combined with his emotional and physical exhaustion, nearly brought Abel to his knees. *This can't be.*

While Abel fought to stay upright, he also fought the all too familiar pains of abandonment he'd known would consume him when Cullen eventually moved on. For now, he was holding them at bay, but he wouldn't be able to do it indefinitely. He still had hope.

Maybe I'm on the wrong dock. Abel looked around the marina, still in disbelief, hoping above all hope he'd taken a wrong turn in his haste to get to Cullen. But no such luck. The boats that had been on either side of *T-Time* were still there, bobbing gently in the waves.

On unsteady legs, Abel ran to the fuel dock. No *T-Time.* He ran to the pumpout station. No *T-Time. He's gone! He's really gone.*

Abel mechanically patted his pocket for his cell phone but remembered he'd put it in the cardboard box with the others. *Damn, Abel!* It belonged to the church anyway, so there was no need to go back for it.

Feeling helpless, Abel walked slowly back up the dock and sat on the steps of the office. He looked at his watch and then looked at the hours of operation affixed to the glass door. *Damn! They don't open for another forty-five minutes.* But a white envelope stuck in the door caught his eye. He looked closely, and Cullen's slip number was written on the outside of the envelope. He glanced around to make sure he was alone and quickly retrieved the envelope and opened it.

> *Dear Hank,*
> *I've decided to move on to Charleston for the*
> *rest of the winter. You guys have been great, and*
> *I appreciate everything you and your staff did to*

make my stay in Southport a good one. You have my
credit card on file and my permission to charge any
remaining balance, and you have my cell if you need
me for anything else.
    Thanks again,
    Cullen Kiley
    T-Time
    Slip C-24

Abel breathed a sigh of relief, folded up the letter again, slipped it back into the envelope, and shoved it under the door. *At least you know where he is. Now what are you gonna do about it?* Abel took his time walking home. There was no rush, and he needed time to think.

Why did Cullen leave? Did it have something to do with the intervention? Had Agnes butted her big nose into his business and told Cullen what was going on? They had worked him relentlessly last night, so he wouldn't put it past Agnes to work Cullen as well. It was definitely a possibility.

Abel hadn't consciously made up his mind, but *if* he decided to drive to Charleston, he could be there in less than four hours. Cullen had told him the trip to Charleston by boat on the outside, as he'd called it—meaning in the ocean—was just under eight hours. But if he went on the inside and followed the Intracoastal Waterway, it was a two-day trip.

When Cullen got home, he fired up his laptop. He searched for every marina between Southport and Charleston and printed the contact information of each. Next he went to Google and typed in "marine forecast." Something called NOAA came up as the first site, so he clicked on it. It asked for a region, which he chose, and then provided a marine weather forecast. Winds out of the SSE at ten knots, seas one to two feet.

"That doesn't seem so bad," Abel said out loud. "I'm gonna bet he went on the outside."

Abel closed his laptop and sighed. "Time to pack." Two hours later, Abel had packed his Honda Accord with what few belongings he had. It was mostly clothes and shoes, jammed in on top of his stereo, computer, and printer. It was amazing how few roots he'd put down here, almost like he knew he was only passing through. When he was done loading the car, Abel locked the front door and slipped the key through the mail slot. He turned around and gasped to find Dottie was standing on his porch. How had he not heard her walk up the stairs?

"Abel?"

"Oh! Hi, Dottie."

Dottie looked at his packed car and back at him. "What's going on?"

"I resigned from the church today, Dottie."

"Why?"

Abel hesitated, trying to decide the right way to handle this. Of course he settled on the truth. "You're probably going to hear sooner or later, Dottie, so I'll just save a stop on the gossip train. I'm gay."

It felt good to say the words to someone other than Cullen. "I'm gay, Dottie," he said again.

"I heard you the first time, Abel. But what does that have to do with you quitting the church?"

"You know the church's beliefs about homosexuality. Pastor Williams thought it best if I move on."

"Are you fucking kidding me?" Dottie said, surprising the hell out of Abel.

"Dottie!" he said.

"I'm sorry for my language, Abel, but that dinosaur of a pastor has really gone and pissed me off this time. What hypocrites!"

"Hypocrites? What do you mean?"

"Abel, if you knew half the stories running around town about the Pastor and *his wife*, you wouldn't believe it."

"What stories?" Abel asked, identifying the shock in his voice.

"I'm not a gossip, Abel, but I hear things. And apparently the Pastor's prostate cancer treatment a few years ago left him impotent, and it's pretty common knowledge that since then, Agnes has been carrying on with Burt Townsend every time the pastor leaves town."

"What? Burt Townsend? That widower who lives on Nash Avenue?"

"That's him! But yet they send you away because you're gay?"

"Technically I resigned. But if I hadn't, they would have fired me anyway."

"Those bigots," she hissed. "Abel. Please reconsider?"

"But what about the congregation?" Abel asked. "Wouldn't they have a problem with this?"

"Some of the old schoolers who aren't as hip as I am might. But they make up such a small part of the congregation now. Especially since you've brought so many young people and life into our little church. Abel, you're the best associate pastor we've ever had, and I don't want you to go."

Abel swallowed the lump bobbing up and down in his throat and threw his arms around Dottie's neck. "Thank you. I had no idea you felt that way. I thought everyone loved Pastor Williams."

"Oh shoot, Abel, everyone simply tolerates him. Did you not notice how many more people there were in church yesterday? That was all because you were in the pulpit. Wonderful sermon, by the way."

"Thank you. You have no idea how much all this means to me."

"Well, you deserve it, and I'm sorry I haven't told you how much we appreciate you before now. We all just assumed you knew."

"It's okay, Dottie. It's been that way all my life. Everyone apparently just assumed I knew."

"Oh, Abel." Dottie kissed his cheek. "You will be missed. But if you wanna stay, I know I can get more than half the congregation to stand up for you. Of course you know the archaic rules of the church. You couldn't be open with your lifestyle, but you would still have your job. And more importantly, we would still have you."

"Thank you, Dottie, but the job here is not that important to me. I will miss you and some of the congregation, but I'm tired of living a lie. I've hidden this all my life, and I'm done with that."

Dottie dipped her head. "I wish it wasn't like this, Abel. I wish everyone could just be loved for who they are. But things are changing. However slowly. It may not happen in my lifetime, but you'll see it. I'm sure of it." She hesitated. "Do you know where you're going to settle?"

"Not sure. Right now I'm headed to Charleston, and if everything works out the way I'm hoping, I may settle in New England come the spring."

"I wish you all the best, and I hope this all has something to do with that handsome Reverend Kiley."

"It certainly does. And thank you, Dottie. You've been a great friend."

Dottie smiled warmly, squeezed both of Abel's hands, and kissed him on the cheek again. "You be happy, son."

"I'll do my best." Abel bounced down the steps, hopped in his car, and pulled away from the curb with renewed hope.

After stopping at the local Radio Shack, where Abel picked up a prepaid cell phone, he drove along Hwy 17 and dialed every marina in Myrtle Beach. Cullen had told him that was the halfway point to Charleston, and he wanted to see if there were any reservations for *T-Time* in case Cullen did travel along the Intracoastal. But he struck out on every call, which wasn't necessarily a bad thing.

Next he moved on to Charleston proper. There were only a handful of marinas in Charleston Harbor, so Abel started with the A's. He called the Ashley Marina. No reservation there. Next was the Charleston City Marina, and lo and behold…. Abel smiled broadly when the dock master said they had a reservation for a boat named *T-Time*, and it was scheduled to arrive between three and four o'clock.

Cullen! You may send me packing, but I'll never know unless I take the chance.

CHAPTER SEVENTEEN

WITH A heavy heart, Cullen sat at *T-Time*'s helm in the middle of the Atlantic Ocean, with nothing in sight but glistening water in every direction. The seas were calm. The winds and current were favorable, and *T-Time* was on autopilot with a course set for the inlet to Charleston Harbor.

With such good conditions, there was nothing to keep Cullen's mind off of Abel. And damn if he didn't have another seven hours of *nothingness* until he reached Charleston. That would give him plenty of time to second-guess every decision he'd made in the last year and a half. Starting with his leaving Southport and Abel behind.

On more than one occasion, his hands were on the wheel and about to change course and head back to Southport. But why? What good would that do him? He had no idea where Abel was. And even if he did, would Abel want to see him? On one hand he felt like he was deserting Abel, but on the other hand, if what Agnes said was true and Abel wanted him to go, he had to respect his wishes. Either way, going back now wouldn't get him the answers he needed.

At one point Cullen thought about contacting the Southport authorities, but there was the simple question of whether the church had done anything legally wrong. Cullen had no doubt they had acted unethically, but there was no penalty by law for that. But what if Abel hadn't been coerced into going into that horrible therapy? What if he went willfully?

A chill ran up Cullen's spine when he remembered what he'd read about the methods used in that particular therapy. Prior to the 1980s, some of the methods included masturbatory reconditioning through electric shock applications to the genitals, and nausea-inducing drugs and prolonged ice baths administered simultaneously with the presentation of homoerotic stimuli.

Luckily for Abel, after 1981, clinical techniques used in the U.S. had been mostly limited to counseling, visualization, social skills training, psychoanalytic therapy, and spiritual interventions such as prayer and support groups. But Cullen also remembered there were still some reports of aversive treatments by unlicensed practitioners.

He decided that, as soon as he got to Charleston, he would try to look up conversion therapy facilities in upstate North Carolina to see what he could find, but he also knew with today's HIPAA laws, no one would give him any information about whether Abel had actually been admitted. But he would at least know if the clinic or facility was a reputable one.

As the hours passed, Cullen checked and rechecked his instruments, making sure he was still on course and everything was as it should be. He looked at his radar for any blips indicating another vessel in the vicinity, but within a fifty-mile radius, he saw nothing but a blank screen. It was just Cullen, his boat, and the sea, but he didn't feel uneasy or alone. In fact, like most times when he was at sea, he felt deeply spiritual. With the beauty of the vast ocean surrounding him, how could he question what God had created? But that had been when he wasn't worrying about Abel.

Even with Abel front and center in his reflections, he still thought a lot about his faith. How he'd turned his back on God, all under the premise that God had turned his back on him. The more he searched his soul, the more he realized that yes, God had taken Cole from him, but he wouldn't have even known Cole if God hadn't brought Cole to him. A Bible verse from Job 1:21 suddenly came to mind: "Naked I came from my mother's womb, and naked shall I return there. The Lord gave and the Lord has taken away; blessed be the name of the Lord."

Cullen felt the urge to raise his hands to the heavens, something he hadn't really done since he'd left the church. But instead he started by openly acknowledging how selfish he'd been for focusing solely on his loss instead of feeling grateful for the time they'd had.

In their nine short years together, they'd experienced more love and joy than many people get in a lifetime. Because of Cole, for the first time in Cullen's life, he had loved completely and felt loved unconditionally, and that was something many people, like Abel, never got to experience.

Additionally Cole had died doing something he absolutely loved. At the hospital the doctors had assured Cullen that Cole had not suffered anything more than a flash of a headache before he dropped, another way Cole had been so lucky. Many people suffer long illnesses and slow painful deaths, and Cole had suffered neither. *Haven't we all prayed for the Lord to have mercy on us when our time came and take us quickly and painlessly?* God had given that to Cole.

Cullen sat back in his captain's chair, linked his fingers together, and laid them across his chest. *How could I have missed all of these blessings? Was I so blinded with grief that I blocked everything else out completely?*

Hypocrite was the first word that came to mind. Over the years, he'd counseled so many grieving loved ones about the will of God and his plan, but when it came time to put his money where his mouth was, he'd failed miserably. *If this was a test, you seriously blew it, man.*

Cullen was startled out of his thoughts by the beeping sound of his autopilot. He silenced the alarm and looked at his GPS display. The message was flashing. "You have arrived at your destination."

What? Cullen looked up, and he could clearly see the rock jetty marking the inlet to the Charleston Harbor just about a mile ahead. *I can't believe I'm here already.* He looked at his watch: 3:15. Where had the time gone?

Cullen pulled back on the throttle, slowed to idle speed, and left the helm to ready his lines. When his bow, stern, and midship lines were secure and set, he returned to the helm. He entered the jetty and followed the channel markers into the harbor. Fort Sumter was standing regally off of his port bow, and as he passed it by, he actually surprised himself by saying a quick prayer for all the people who had lost their lives there during the Civil War.

To Cullen's right the amazing Cooper River Bridge loomed large and grand in the distance. To his left was the more understated Ashley River, and straight ahead was the historic Charleston Battery.

Taking in the scenery before him, Cullen acknowledged hundreds of church steeples dotting the Charleston skyline, and the sight tugged insistently at his heart. He'd read somewhere that Charleston had over four hundred places of worship. *They don't call Charleston the "Holy City" for nothing.*

Cullen radioed the marina with his arrival, and they had assigned him a slip just inside the megadock, across from the

Carolina Queen paddle-wheeler. He couldn't actually see the dock or his slip until he rounded the paddle-wheeler's bow, but when he did, his jaw dropped.

Is that? Could that be? Jesus! It is!

The sun was shining off golden locks that could only belong to Abel. He was standing next to the dockhand in all his gorgeous glory. They locked eyes instantly, and Cullen felt a broad smile spread across his face. His swelling heart started beating rapidly against his ribcage and, if left unattended, would no doubt have leapt out of his chest.

Cullen! You have to stay in control just long enough to dock this boat and then you can freak out all you want. But not now!

Cullen did stay in control. He fought the ebbing tides and swift currents and maneuvered *T-Time* right up to the dock so Abel and the dockhand could reach the already set lines and secure them to the cleats. When he shut off the engines, he whispered, "Thank you, God." For safe passage and for Abel.

CHAPTER EIGHTEEN

ABEL HAD made the trip to Charleston with anticipation, excitement, and yes, trepidation. He'd arrived just before three o'clock, and he was as nervous as he'd ever been. Not having any idea how he would be received had almost been his undoing. But if he hadn't given this a shot, he would have wondered for the rest of his life.

He would not have wondered about his feelings because he already knew how he felt about Cullen. But the big question was, how did Cullen feel about him? He sensed Cullen cared about him, but was Cole's memory still too raw for Cullen even to consider another relationship? As he pulled into the Charleston City Marina parking lot, Abel knew he would have all the answers to his questions very soon.

If Cullen didn't want him, he would get back into his car and drive until he found a place that suited him. Atlanta, maybe. Or he'd heard nice things about Birmingham, Alabama. But he tried not to think about those possibilities yet. Leaving Cullen behind was his last resort.

After making his way to the dock master's office, Abel found out to which boat slip *T-Time* would be assigned and followed their directions to find it.

As it turned out, Cullen's slip was directly across from a huge old paddle-wheeler, and Abel couldn't see around it, so he had no way of knowing when Cullen would arrive. Abel paced up and down the dock nervously until a dockhand showed up and said Cullen would be there any minute.

Abel started to tremble slightly. His breathing increased, and if he wasn't careful, he was afraid he'd start hyperventilating right there on the dock. He placed his hand over his stomach and pressed in an attempt to steady it from the continuous backflips happening deep inside of his abdomen. But instead of settling, they intensified, making him almost nauseated.

"There he is." The dockhand pointed as *T-Time* rounded the front of the paddle-wheeler, and Cullen's face slowly came into view. He and Cullen locked eyes for one instant, and Abel knew. He released the breath he was holding. The smile on Cullen's face told him everything he needed to know. He had his answer. He was finally home.

Abel couldn't stand still. He was bouncing from one foot to the other and had to stick his hands in his pockets to keep them from waving continuously.

Cullen, on the other hand, had docking to worry about. Not to mention dealing with other boats and currents. But from the smile on his face, he was having just as hard a time concentrating as Abel.

As ever the master captain, Cullen gingerly brought the boat up to the dock, and Abel grabbed the bowline and held it as the dockhand grabbed the midship and stern lines and secured the boat to the cleats.

When the roar of the engines faded into silence, the lack of sound made Abel's thoughts go wild and a little doubtful. But when he and Cullen locked eyes for the second time, he was again solid. Grounded. Abel hoped his own expression conveyed every emotion he was feeling, but in actuality, how could it?

It must have given Cullen enough of a glimpse because in two seconds flat, Cullen was down the stairs, onto the dock, and standing ten feet in front of Abel, his dazzling blue eyes gazing lovingly into Abel's.

Abel wanted to go to him, but his feet felt like lead. He couldn't move. He wanted his arms around Cullen, but he was too terrified to go to him.

The dockhand took the unsecured bowline from Abel's hand, wrapped it around the cleat, and walked back to Cullen. "Can I help you with the electric and water?"

"No, thanks. I've got it." Cullen handed the man something, probably a tip, and the man said thanks and hurried away to assist the next boater.

Cullen found Abel's eyes again, and they held each other's gaze for a very long moment.

Cullen was the first to speak. "I thought I'd lost you."

Abel found the will to take one step closer to Cullen. "Not a chance."

Cullen matched his step. "But Agnes said you sent her to ask me to leave Southport."

Abel took another step, lessening the gap between them still more. "She lied. I could never ask you to leave. I love you too much for that."

Cullen matched his step again.

"But Agnes said Pastor Williams drove you upstate for conversion therapy."

"She lied again. I never left Southport until I followed you here."

One last step and Abel launched himself into Cullen's arms. Burying his face in Cullen's neck, Abel inhaled deeply. Home.

Cullen lifted Abel off of the ground and spun him around. When he next spoke, his voice was low and full of disdain. "We were played, Abel."

"It appears that way," Abel said. "But they gambled and lost. And they'll answer for it someday."

"Can we get off this dock now?"

"Please," Abel said.

"I need to hook up the water and the power before we run the batteries down. Wanna help?"

"Aye, aye, Captain." Abel brought his hand to his forehead in a mock salute.

Cullen's laugh was as hearty a laugh as Abel had ever heard escape the man's lips, and it warmed him to his core.

Minutes later both men kicked off their shoes, and Abel climbed down the stairs to the saloon with Cullen right behind him.

"Abel." Cullen grabbed Abel by the arm and spun him around. He covered Abel's lips in a crushing kiss, and when he moaned against Abel's mouth, Abel opened to him. Cullen's kiss was insatiable. He tasted like everything Abel loved in this world. Everything Abel would ever need.

Abel was still in the same clothes he'd worn to church the day before, his tie now hanging loosely around his neck. As Cullen kissed him, Abel felt Cullen's hand sliding the tie through his shirt collar and tossing it aside. Cullen ripped Abel's dress shirt apart at the chest, and Abel heard buttons ricochet against windows and cabinetry. Cullen broke their kiss just long enough to pull Abel's white T-shirt over his head.

"Don't." Cullen kissed him again. "Ever." Another kiss. "Leave." A third kiss. "Me."

"I want to explain," Abel whispered.

"Later!"

Cullen pulled his sweatshirt over his head, took Abel by the hand, and led him to his cabin. When they stepped through the door, Cullen spun Abel around and pinned him to the door. "I need you, Abel. I want you to claim me. I want you inside me."

Abel spun Cullen around, raised Cullen's arms over his head, and held his wrists tightly, pinning him against the door. When their lips met again, they both gasped into each other's mouths. The warmth and wetness drove Abel mad with desire.

He'd wanted this. Waited for this. But Cullen had never seemed ready. Abel had always thought Cole had claimed that part of Cullen and had taken it with him, but now Cullen was asking him for it. Needing it from him. And begging him for it.

Abel broke their kiss, and Cullen moaned in protest. But Abel ignored him and licked his way down Cullen's chin to his neck, where he delivered soft wet kisses over his shoulder before lowering his attentions and burying his face in Cullen's warm armpit, first one and then the other, inhaling and licking the scent he so desperately craved.

Focusing his kisses elsewhere, Abel dropped even lower to Cullen's chest. There he teased Cullen's nipples, biting and sucking, drawing gasps from Cullen and then licking and soothing away the obvious sting. Releasing Cullen's wrists, Abel dropped lower and licked his way down Cullen's torso, following the line of hair that always intrigued him until he was on his knees and face to face with the bulge in Cullen's jeans.

Abel slapped his hand on top of Cullen's bulge and squeezed it tightly, grabbing Cullen's ass with his other hand and kneading it. Abel's tongue was lodged inside of Cullen's navel as he worked Cullen from both ends until Cullen was gyrating and trembling beneath his touch.

Cullen sucked in a ragged breath when Abel snaked his hand down the front of Cullen's jeans and rubbed the moist head of Cullen's cock with the tip of a callused finger. Cullen stiffened, and his cock jumped at Abel's touch. Cullen grew visibly harder as Abel released the buttons of his fly one at a time, until Cullen's jeans were hanging open and the outline of Cullen's length was visible through his black boxer briefs.

Abel yanked Cullen's jeans to his ankles, and Cullen stepped out of them and kicked them to the side. Abel stood and, in a herculean move that surprised even him, lifted Cullen's six-foot two-inch frame into his arms like he was a ragdoll and carried him to the bed.

When Abel set Cullen down on the bed, Cullen's eyes were wide with obvious surprise. He smiled at Abel and shook his head.

"You continue to amaze me," Cullen whispered.

"And I intend on doing that for the rest of our lives."

Cullen sat up and pulled Abel between his open legs. He unbuckled Abel's belt, unfastened his black dress pants, and let them fall to the floor. Abel stepped out of his pants and brought a foot up to remove his sock when Cullen slapped his hand away. "Me."

Abel laughed quietly as Cullen peeled his black sock off and tossed it to the floor and then lifted the other foot and did the same. Clad in nothing now but his underwear, Abel shoved Cullen to his back and straddled Cullen's chest.

Cullen pulled the waistband of Abel's briefs down, exposing Abel's hard length, the head already glistening with his excitement. He stuck his tongue out and licked the juice lingering there, earning a loud gasp from Abel. Abel lifted up to his knees, and Cullen pulled Abel's underwear as far down as he could, Abel giving him clear access to what he seemed to want so desperately.

Cullen swallowed Abel to the back of his throat and held him there, Abel trembling from the sensation, and then slid his mouth back up and down again, taking Abel's breath away. Cullen squeezed and juggled Abel's balls with one hand while he worked his mouth and hand up and down Abel's length over and over, until Abel felt his balls tightening and pulled away before he lost his release on the spot.

Abel slid down the bed and knelt between Cullen's legs. He pulled Cullen's underwear down and off and buried his face in Cullen's crotch. Cullen's masculine scent filled his nostrils to capacity, the scent seemingly even more intense than usual. He took Cullen into his mouth and worked him up and down, focusing on the sensitive area under the head, stopping only to suck and nibble on Cullen's balls, tossing them around in his mouth and releasing them.

Abel hadn't been sexually active for all that long, but he was a quick learner. He'd been trying to master everything Cullen had done to him during the first few times they'd been together, and with each encounter, he felt more and more confident in his abilities. But he was about to embark on a totally new experience. He'd never been inside anyone before, and he was a little bit nervous. Cullen had been so patient with him, and he kept telling himself that all he could do was to try his best to remember everything Cullen had done, and he would be okay. Maybe not perfect, but okay.

Cullen must have sensed his apprehension. "Stop worrying. I can see it in your eyes."

"Sorry," Abel said. "I want this to be good for you."

"It will be good for me because it's you, Abel. You are good for me."

With Cullen's words, Abel felt a new sense of confidence. He lifted Cullen's legs over his head, and Cullen took them from there. Abel used both his hands to hold Cullen's cheeks apart and ran his tongue over Cullen's opening. The taste was so sweet, Abel couldn't help but linger—licking, probing, and sucking, and then doing it all over again. Abel's actions were relaxing Cullen. He could feel Cullen loosening up with each probe of his tongue.

Abel licked his index finger and pressed it against Cullen's hole. Cullen moaned and shuddered under him. He took that as a sign and pushed his finger in just until he felt resistance, and then he retreated. Cullen bucked and pushed against him, so Abel pressed all the way in, past the muscle and as far as his finger would go. He pulled out just a little and moved his finger around, searching for the little bump that every time Cullen rubbed against inside him drove him absolutely crazy. He moved his finger a couple more times and felt it at the same time as Cullen hissed and arched his back.

"Oh my God," Cullen said as Abel moved his finger back and forth over the little bump that was the prostate.

Cullen whimpered and gasped as he squirmed under Abel's attentions. As Abel fingered Cullen, he watched his expression of absolute abandon, and he knew Cullen was truly giving himself over to him. And Abel loved the sounds escaping Cullen's lips, driving him ever so close to his own release.

Withdrawing his finger, Abel laughed at Cullen's moans of protest. "Where's the lubricant, Mr. Impatient?"

"In the drawer," Cullen said in a rich but hoarse voice that didn't sound like his own.

Abel found what he was after and squeezed some lube onto his fingers. He warmed the liquid and then rubbed it generously around Cullen's opening, making sure he was slick with the stuff. Then Abel gingerly slid two fingers inside Cullen and again honed in on that special spot. When Abel found it this time, he wiggled his two fingers, and Cullen wailed, threw his head back, and literally came up off of the bed.

"Oh God, Abel. Need–you–in–side–me–now."

Abel withdrew his fingers, made sure his dick was slick with lube, and stared down nervously at the hole he was about to violate. Without any further hesitation, Abel pressed his length against Cullen's opening and pushed in slowly. Cullen hissed, rested his legs on Abel's shoulders, and dropped his arms to Abel's thighs, where he momentarily held him at bay. The instant Abel felt Cullen's warm heat gripping him, he had to fight the urge to shove all the way in. But he knew he needed to give Cullen time to adjust to the intrusion.

Cullen sighed deeply and pulled Abel in a little deeper. A few more movements and Abel looked down to find he was totally sheathed inside Cullen's tight ass. With Cullen's encouragement, Abel withdrew slowly and then pushed back inside in several slow delicious thrusts. Abel needed to see better. To see more. He rose up onto his knees and took Cullen by the ankles. He held Cullen's legs up and apart and watched himself moving in, his length totally disappearing inside of Cullen and then reappearing.

Taking himself in hand, Cullen mirrored Abel's movement. When Abel looked at Cullen again, his eyes were closed and his head was thrown back in complete abandon.

As Abel steadily moved in and out of him, he could feel Cullen's hot, velvety insides surrounding him, encompassing him with each thrust. The way they fit together, the way Cullen's body gripped him, made Abel intensely aware of just how much he loved the man. Abel felt like Cullen was plundering his heart, and to see this look on Cullen's face again and again, he would gladly let him have it.

Abel knew at that moment he would protect Cullen at all costs. He was so worth protecting. Worth fighting for. *They* were worth fighting for.

Feeling his release start at the tip of his toes, Abel picked up his pace. "Cullen!"

"Let it go, baby. I want to feel your release inside me. Mark me. Make me your own."

With those words pushing him over the edge, Abel quickened his thrusts and lost all conscious thought. At that exact moment in time, he chose to let go of every bad thing that had ever happened to him in his life. He released it all to God and the universe and then, for the first time as his release coursed through him, gave in to the waves of sweet pleasure unobstructed by old dark memories.

He was pumping feverishly when the sound of Cullen's moans brought him back to reality. A reality that was somehow different now. New. Clean. And no longer soiled like it had been before this revelation.

Cullen's free hand was guiding him, pulling him in deeper and harder until his own release was covering his chest and abdomen in long, drawn-out spasms. When they were both drained and exhausted, Abel slid out of Cullen and collapsed at his side.

Still breathing heavily, Abel got up and retrieved a warm cloth. He cleaned Cullen from top to bottom, then crawled back into bed and snuggled up against him.

"You were incredible," Cullen said. "That was one of the most intense experiences of my life."

"Somehow all this has changed me," Abel admitted.

Cullen rose up on his elbow and rested his head in his hand. "How so?"

"I'm not totally sure, but I just know I'm different. All the unfortunate things that have happened to me in my life—things that I've held on to forever—are fading away. Almost like I've released them somehow. I no longer feel dirty and ashamed of who I was, who I am. The unwanted, insecure kid with no family. It's all going away, and I have you to thank for that. You awakened me, Cullen. I was too afraid to say it before now, but I love you, Cullen Kiley."

Cullen pulled Abel close to him. "I'm ashamed to say I've been such a coward. I've been too afraid to admit things to you, to myself even, fearing that having feelings for you meant they would replace the love I had for Cole. But no more. Now I know God and Cole had a hand in all of this. In my dreams Cole handed me off to you. Not just because you needed me, but because I also needed you. You say I awakened you? Abel, you have single-handedly renewed my faith in God and literally brought me back to the land of the living, and I will love you forever for it."

CHAPTER NINETEEN

CULLEN AND Abel were sitting side by side on the couch, feet propped up on an ottoman, sipping bourbon and listening to a little music.

"So let me get this straight," Abel said. "Agnes out and out lied to you and said I sent her to ask you to leave town while at the same time her husband and his cronies were holding me hostage and trying to convince me to submit to conversion therapy?"

"And we're the sinners?" Cullen chuckled.

"Apparently." Abel took a sip of his bourbon, something for which he was acquiring quite a taste, and swirled it around in his mouth. He swallowed. "Oh man, I forgot to tell you this."

"What?"

"After I'd packed my car and was about to leave the church residence, I ran into my neighbor Dottie. She asked if I was leaving and if so, why. For the first time in my life, I said the words. 'Because I'm gay.' She blew a gasket."

"Bigoted old woman," Cullen cursed.

"No. She was on my side," Abel clarified. "She didn't want me to go and said she knew more than half the church would stand up for me if I wanted to stay. Apparently a large part of the congregation hates the Williamses."

"Get out," Cullen said. "Seriously?"

"Dottie says the pastor and the missus are not what they appear to be." Abel filled Cullen in on everything Dottie had told him.

"That two-faced old...," Cullen said. "She's cheating on her poor impotent husband, and she says we're gonna burn in hell?"

Abel frowned. "God will repay each person according to what they have done."

"Romans 2:6," Cullen said.

"You're good." Abel squeezed Cullen's knee. "But you know the thing Dottie said that shocked me more than anything?"

"What's that?"

"The fact that more than half the church would have stood up for me. More than half, Cullen! That's huge."

"That's a testament to you and the way you've reached people there." Cullen laid his hand over Abel's heart. "I think the world is changing, Abel. Even for the Southern Baptists. Hatred is taught, and the teachers, the old-timers, are dying off. And they're taking the fire and brimstone with them. As young people find the church, they bring with them an openness to love others unconditionally. And in my opinion, that will in itself have a big impact on all religions."

"I hope you're right."

"Would you want to go back? To your old position, I mean?"

"Absolutely not. If I did, we would need to hide our love, and I won't do that. We can't live in a bubble. I love you, and I want the world to know it."

Just then Cullen heard Tracy Byrd's voice filling the saloon with one of his favorite songs on his playlist. It was about a man thanking the keeper of the stars for bringing him the person he loved and joining their two hearts. Cullen held up his glass for a toast. "To the keeper of the stars, for bringing our two hearts together. I love you, Abel." Cullen stood and offered his hand. "Dance with me."

Abel hesitated. "I don't know how."

"You mean you've never danced before?"

Abel shrugged. "It's frowned upon in my religion."

"And how do you feel about that?" Cullen asked.

"Well, I've never seen any verse that prohibits dancing. In fact, just the opposite. David and Moses 'danced for joy' in the Bible. And one particular verse I remember was in Psalms. 'Let them praise His name with the dance: Let them sing praises to Him with the timbrel and harp.'"

Cullen nodded. "And don't forget 2 Samuel 6:14, 'Then David danced before the Lord with all his might,'" Cullen added. "Hell, there are at least six I can think of off the top of my head that mention dancing favorably." Cullen still had his hand out. "So will you?"

"If you don't make fun of me," Abel said, getting to his feet.

"Never."

"What do I do?"

Cullen pulled Abel close to him, took Abel's right hand in his left, and wrapped his right arm around Abel's waist. "Just follow my lead and get lost in the music."

Abel rested his head on Cullen's shoulder and closed his eyes. He felt Cullen's muscles moving, contracting and releasing, guiding him, and after a few minutes, he was following Cullen effortlessly as Cullen turned him and swayed. Before long he *was* lost in the music. Lost in the man that was Cullen Kiley.

"I love this," Abel whispered. "I get to hold you and be close to you just like when we're in bed. Shoot, it's almost as good as having sex."

"Seriously?"

"I said *almost*. Now shut up and spin me again."

"You sure are a bossy back lead."

Epilogue

Cullen looked up to the sky and let the warm spring sun beat down on his face. He and Abel had been back in P-town just over a month, and today was Easter Sunday, his first official Sunday leading the mass at the Church of Saint Mary of the Harbor.

Since their return Abel had already met with the Bishop and the Diocesan on Ministry to start the process of becoming an ordained Episcopal priest and was scheduled to begin his continuing education in two weeks. Until then, he would act as a deacon of the church and learn as much as he could before his formal education began.

This, of course, was only the first step for Abel. He was learning to truly accept himself and his ability to serve God in a welcoming and nonjudgmental environment. Cullen could already see subtle changes in Abel's self-esteem and the way he was beginning to come to terms with and move past his childhood and his issues of abandonment and self-worth.

With each passing day, Cullen fell a little more in love with the man who'd saved him and wholeheartedly supported him in whatever direction he chose to take with his calling. But more importantly, Abel seemed extremely happy to be embarking on this journey with Cullen beside him. They had become a true team in every way.

Cullen was a nervous wreck pacing outside on the church steps, wondering if his parishioners would truly embrace him and welcome him back or simply go through the motions.

It had taken him and Abel weeks to write his first sermon, and it centered on the hypocrisy of the clergy. But more so about his hypocrisy—the loss of love, grieving, giving up on life and God, and then when he least expected it, finding love again and being, in a sense, reborn.

It was literally his and Abel's story in a sermon format, and there were just as many of Abel's words in the lesson as his. He loved it even more because of that. Cullen hoped the sermon would help explain some of the reason he'd had to leave the church so abruptly.

Some parishioners knew, of course, but others had no clue, nor did the newer church members, so it was make-or-break time. But all Cullen could do was be honest and heartfelt, and in doing that he would have to wear his heart on his sleeve and give them everything he had to give. If they didn't accept him back, he would move to another church, knowing he'd given it all he had.

Cullen heard the processional music and took his position at the rear of the church behind the acolyte carrying the cross. He followed his cue and made his way slowly down the aisle, listening to the magnificence of the pipe organ, nodding and smiling to familiar faces, but mostly just taking it all in.

The church was decorated with thousands of spring flowers, so colorful it almost hurt the eyes, and the sun was beaming through the stained-glass windows behind the altar, sending rays of additional colors streaming through the entire church. In that very moment, he wondered how he could have ever left something so beautiful. Something he loved so much.

When the procession stopped, Cullen knelt to give thanks and then proceeded to his position behind the altar. He stopped and glanced out over the church and the congregation. Abel was proudly seated in the first row, next to Elaina, and Cullen's eyes suddenly filled with tears. Through his tears he saw the shadow of Cole sitting on the other side of Abel, smiling broadly. Before he could find the words to speak, the entire church rose to their feet and started clapping.

Cullen wiped the tears away with his robe. He went to Abel, offered him his hand, and led him to the front of the church. The two men stood with the entire congregation applauding them. When the applause was over, Cullen pulled Abel into a tight embrace and whispered into his ear.

"Now we are home."

SCOTTY CADE left Corporate America and twenty-five years of marketing and public relations in 2004 to buy an inn & restaurant on the island of Martha's Vineyard with Kell, his husband of over twenty years.

He started writing stories as soon as he could read, but only in the last five years for publication. When not at the inn, you can find him on the bow of his boat writing romance novels with his Shetland sheepdog, Mavis, at his side. Being from the South and a lover of commitment and fidelity, all of his characters find their way to long, healthy relationships, however long it takes them to get there. He believes that, in the end, the boy should always get the boy.

Scotty and Kell are avid boaters and live aboard their boat, spending the summers on Martha's Vineyard and winters in various locations down south.

Website: www.scottycade.com
Facebook: www.facebook.com/scotty.cade
Twitter: @ScottyCade
E-mail: scotty@scottycade.com

Forever
FOR NOW

SCOTTY CADE

Leeland Jeffers is a contented single man with a thriving career in Atlanta. He's had a few unsuccessful relationships over the years, but no one has even come close to his first love, Harrison Rhinehart. They met in college when a mutual friend, Suzie Garrison, introduced Harry into their close-knit group. When the supposedly "straight" Harry made a move on Lee, the two men entered into a tumultuous secret love affair. In their senior year, the relationship finally ended when Harry informed Lee he was marrying Suzie.

Since graduation, the college friends have drifted apart. However, an unexpected invitation to a destination wedding seems set to reunite them all. Lee's speculation on whether Harry and Suzie will make an appearance threatens to derail his attendance. But Lee decides the hell with it and makes plans to go, Harry Rhinehart or no Harry Rhinehart.

www.dreamspinnerpress.com

Two cadets from very different worlds.
One forbidden love.

KNOBS

SCOTTY CADE

Angus Conrad (Gus) McRae is a privileged Charlestonian following family tradition and attending the Citadel, harboring big dreams of a military career. With the infamous Hell Week behind him, he quickly realizes being a Knob (a freshman cadet) is just as tough—especially for a man like Gus who must keep his sexuality a secret. Then a sudden dorm reassignment lands him with a roommate in the form of one of the football team's top players—working-class jock Stewart Adam (Sam) Morley—and life gets increasingly complicated.

Gus can't imagine a man like Sam as gay, yet there's something between them—exchanged glances, the occasional innuendo. Sexual tensions rise, leaving them more than friends but less than lovers. Gus and Sam know there's too much to lose and they must keep their attraction hidden. If they fail, they risk destroying their hopes and dreams for a prosperous future in a military world that's not yet ready to accommodate masculine gay men.

www.dreamspinnerpress.com

SCOTTY CADE

THE ROYAL
STREET
HEIST

Bissonet & Cruz Investigations: Book One

When valuable Civil War era art is stolen from a popular New Orleans gallery, NOPD Lead Detective Montgomery "Beau" Bissonet and his partner set out to solve the crime. When the gallery's insurance company sends Tollison Cruz to the Big Easy to conduct their own independent investigation, personalities clash and battle lines are definitely drawn.

The heist quickly becomes a politically driven high profile case, and Detective Bissonet is furious when he's ordered to work along side Investigator Cruz to assure a timely arrest. The heat index soars to new levels when the two investigators discover they have a lot more in common than originally thought.

With the tension between them temporarily sated, Bissonet and Cruz finally start to work together, on more than just a professional level. But everything comes to a screeching halt when Beau discovers his cohort in crime has been withholding information regarding the investigation and has been concealing a very questionable past. What happens next rivals the scorching summer heat.

www.dreamspinnerpress.com

VEILED
LOYALTIES
BISSONET & CRUZ INVESTIGATIONS

SCOTTY CADE

Sequel to *The Royal Street Heist*
Bissonet & Cruz Investigations: Book Two

Halloween is Beau Bissonet's favorite holiday, from carving pumpkins to decorating his yard to donning a costume and scaring the neighborhood kids. But this year his Halloween is about to take a different turn, one that will challenge his skills as a detective and his commitment to his partner in work and love.

A year since Beau and Tollison solved *The Royal Street Heist*, found love, and formed Bissonet & Cruz Investigations, they are thriving personally and professionally. That is until Tollison's ex, Bastien Andros, shows up out of the blue. Naturally, Beau's suspicious, but two days after Bastien's arrival, he goes missing, and Tollison worries his past may catch up to him.

A mysterious package makes clear who has Bastien and what's at stake. With both Bastien and Beau's lives now at risk, Tollison has only one option: travel to Zurich, Switzerland, secure and deliver the ransom, keep both men safe, and stay true to himself at the same time.

www.dreamspinnerpress.com

www.ingramcontent.com/pod-product-compliance
Lightning Source LLC
Chambersburg PA
CBHW060100260626
47160CB00005B/1732